Don't look at them

By

Tiffany Ngwashi

ISBN-10: 1-947662-03-1
ISBN-13: 978-1-947662-03-2

Library of Congress Catalog Card Number: 2017951464

Chapter One

I hate this. I hate it here; I hate all of this. Davina wrote on her bell worksheet and handed it to the bell work collector, Wendell, as she tapped her pencil against the desk. "You… you forgot to write your name on this." Wendell informed her while he fidgeted with the bottom of his shirt.

Davina never understood why this kid was always so nervous around her. She kept to herself and barely even talked. Nevertheless, Davina rolled her eyes and turned her head the other way. Wendell walked away as Davina glanced around the room, observing her peers, just teens being teens. Jade was using her phone against the class rules yet *again*. Anderson was arguing with Mr. Bills about the grade he received. It was honestly an irritating scene to witness.

Anderson can get loud, especially with Mr. Bills; school counselor gets dialed in these situations, *real fast.* Davina placed her head on the desk, attempting to ignore the noise, but it did not work. *Can someone shut this kid up before I do?* Davina thought as she hit her head against her palms. All she could do was wait for that wonderful bell to ring to free her from her insanity, at least for now.

Finally, the sound of freedom rang throughout Rushmore High, as people came pouring out along with it. Davina made her way to the double doors and exposed herself to the sweet smell of fresh air. She started gazing off into the distance, as she felt a chill of wind pass her entire body.

The leaves were dancing frantically, as she fixed her gaze at the tree directly across from her. She began to walk to her bus, as it pulled up on school grounds. Suddenly, Davina froze in her tracks. Her head began to pound.

Suddenly, four leaves began to float off the ground and spin in circles. Davina's nose started to bleed. She dropped to the floor and unconsciously grabbed her journal from her backpack.

Shaking on the ground, she began to visualize her gut-wrenching experience once again. Her eyes rolled back as she began to uncontrollably write down her thoughts, stabbing down words as her pain drove her.

September 20, nine years back

I was in my room, minding my own business, taking a nap with my Favorite teddy bear. My parents were fighting, *as usual*. I was use to it. But today was different.

Glasses were being thrown, and chairs were being flung across the room, just far enough to hit the outer part of the wall where I was sleeping. It was hell in the Michaelson household. I didn't have to see what was being thrown to know that it was.

I was awakened by the sounds of distress. I sat up in my bed and cradled myself in my soft, warm bed sheets. I studied the back of my wrist. My special birthmark itched more than usual today.

Mom always told me that just because I have a special birthmark does not mean that I'm unusual. However, even with my mom's nurturing words, I still felt like I was.

As I sat up in my bed scratching my wrist, the sounds only got worst. The sounds were a casualty to me. The reaction I heard next wasn't. To my surprise, I heard a loud *CRASH!* I sprang out of my bed and ran out of my room, as my teddy bear lay abandoned on the cold floorboards.

As I fled my room to see what all the commotion was about, I slipped on a warm red liquid. As I attempted to get up, my mother caught my eye. I saw my mother, blood and all, on the floor gasping for air.

My father was behind her. There was blood on his hands, his face was pale, and his eyes appeared hollow. I yelled so loud that I even frightened myself.

As I stood there paralyzed with fear and confusion, my father started to walk over to me with a knife in his hand. I was only six, so what could I do! I'll tell you what I did.

I ran to my room, where I had this oddly shaped knife my mother had given to me, just in case someone broke into *my* room. At the time, I tried to explain to my mom that I was special, that I didn't need a knife for protection, that I had something else.

But I kept it in my room regardless. I dove for the knife, as my father quickly lunged after me. I ran into my closet. Before I could close the door, I felt a sharp pain in my arm. I swiped the knife sharply as soon as I felt the pain. I heard gagging, and I began to scream. What I saw haunts me to this day. I saw these…

"Oh, my gosh, are you okay!" a high, concerned voice squealed at the back of my head. It startled me; I automatically snapped out of it. I quickly put away my journal and wiped the blood from my ears and nose as a tall blonde girl stood behind me.

"Are you sure you do not need me to call the nurse?" I shook my head and continued walking to my bus stop. "Well, in that case, Hi, I am Octavia, I hear you are new here." Octavia extended her hand in front of me, flashing her wide, bright smile.

I looked down at my hands smeared in my own blood and looked back at her. I gave her a questionable look and began to walk away. But sure enough, she followed me and began to speak again. "You have my biology class, right?" She wiped her hair out of her face as the wind did the opposite. "Chemistry honors?" I squinted my eyes and nodded.

"You should be heading home instead of following me, you know," I said without thinking. Octavia smiled and shook her head. "You have *no* idea, do you?" Octavia stopped walking and just stood there.

I glared at her and continued walking. "Go home Octavia; I am not looking for friends," I spoke loudly as I passed her.

"I am the new addition to the foster home you are in, Davina."

I stopped. I turned around and started to observe her. She seemed oddly cheerful for a foster child. I wondered her story. As I stood still thinking, she caught up to me.

"Do you have any pets?" I asked.

Octavia looked at me funny. Then she opened her mouth slowly to answer. "I used to have a pet bird," She continued. "Her name was Wendy."

One day my big sister, got her out of her cage, and then..." Octavia's eyes began to get red, as she rubbed the streaming tears from her eyes.

Is this unidentified human "really" crying? I thought to myself, as I bit my tongue not to say anything. However, sure enough, she continued talking, as I played the part of an interested audience.

She sniffled and continued, "Then she began to hug her, then a hug turned into a squeeze, then a squeeze turned into a *POOF*!" My mouth dropped.

I held back my laughter as she continued talking. "She popped Wendy!"

I must admit. I was a bit shocked by the demented turn this pet story took.

However, I was quite curious how the poor bird looked after her critical *tuff love* incident. All puns intended. I softly laughed and began to rub my forehead. I looked at the floor as the school bus approached the bus ramp.

"Well, it is a good thing that we can't bring in pets anyway, so…" I told her this in the most monotone voice I could showcase now. I shook my head and looked dead at her.

"Don't go into any rooms without me, got that?" The look she shot at me gave me chills. She presented me a faint smile and nodded her head. "Good… glad we understand each other," I softly told her, as the school bus door slammed behind me.

Chapter Two

It has been 12 days since the oxygen breach. **I'm almost on my last box of food. Well, in my section that is. At the moment there _is_ more food on the ship, just not in my section. I'm... I'm almost done boarding the bodies off the ship, but there's just... just so many...**

Mazikeen wiped a warm tear from her cheek and continued. Shaking as she held her journal. **I keep hearing voices in my head again. Even though everybody is dead, I can still hear the thoughts of a young girl wondering if she will ever see her parents again, wondering if she will ever find a way out. You know, she almost sounds like me... what I think about. I need to be strong; I have to find a way out of this.**

Mazikeen put down her journal and began to study her pen. Her thoughts raced as she pictured the endless possibilities of her existence. "Why am I still alive?" She whispered.

"How am I still breathing?" She slowly got up from her chair and walked to the space station door window. Seven bodies lay there, awaiting their departure, as she glanced out into the galaxy.

She began to sat next to the door as she pressed her forehead on the glass. *If only the earth was safe.* Mazikeen thought. "Why did you have to die?" Mazikeen quietly mumbled under her breath as she began to cry. She wasn't crying because she was alone. She was crying because she wasn't.

I woke up in the fetal position in front of bodies, the sight of which startled me for a second. I pressed the *board* button as I watched the door open. One by one, I pushed the bodies out of the spaceship. It sure took long enough; space food gives you hips, believe it or not.

I wiped the sweat from my forehead as the last body went flying out of the space station. *What do I do now?* I walked away from the door and into the game room on the other side of the space station.

It gets lonely at times, but the food makes up for that. The food here is out of this world. *Literally!* As I was walking, I caught a glimpse of myself in one of the wall mirrors. I slowly walked up to my reflection and touched the mirror lightly.

I studied my tan skin and nose freckles along with my narrow eyes and dark, long, pin straight hair. I take after my dad. His Asian facial features resembled mine.

My mother was a strong, beautiful woman. She was a mix between Dominican and Cameroonian, a County in West Africa, and that only enhanced her beauty. I stopped myself from going any further.

The thought of my parents being gone didn't just make me feel alone; it made me feel broken. I slowly backed away from the mirror and made my way to the chess table. I started to play chess by myself.

I moved the horse over as many times as I wanted. No one was there to scold me on how I'm not obeying the rules of the game. I began to place all the pieces in incorrect places. I fixed my gaze on my room, right next to the game room.

I felt that feeling… that off feeling like I was being watched. I itched the birthmark on my wrist. My wrist itched more and more as I connected my brainwaves to the sounds I was hearing.

I carefully got off the couch and crept my way over to my room. As I was slowly approaching my room, a thick mass quickly passed me, but it vanished before I had the option to be frightened. I halted in my tracks, but I understood. I wasn't going crazy; I wasn't imagining things.

This was *real*. I was right all along; I wasn't alone. Every spirit that died 12 days ago on this ship was here, right with me, right beside me as I threw their corpses out of existence, and there's nothing I could do about it.

I quickly sat down on the floor and started to meditate. I attempted to hear the voices I heard earlier.

With every breath I took, I could feel various amounts of energy consuming the air, everything from sorrowful energies to frightened energies to evil energies. My eyes stayed closed because I feared what I would see if I opened them.

As I sat in the middle of the floor, I felt something caress my face. I didn't dare open my eyes. I squeezed my fist and bit my lip. The feeling moved to my neck then to my arms. I still didn't open my eyes; if I did, I don't think I would be able to close them again.

Chapter Three

"Are you ready?" A black woman in exercise attire asked the class, as she hit the play button on her iPod. "Ok then, begin!" The class began to dance as if their lives depended on it. Guess what? **It did.**

If you didn't make this famous dance team in Louisiana, I'm pretty sure you won't find another "The Hip Moment" anywhere else. There are limited dance studios where young people can break dance in this place. Meanwhile, California is a place of infinite opportunities. Dancing schools over there are a big deal.

Klaus already knows people are looking at opportunities in California in his class. But come on! Who is *really* going to convince their parents to move all the way to Cali? He's been there, done that. Pretty sure all these other people have too, so this dance group is all they have left.

Why isn't the boy in the back dancing? I thought to myself, as I chewed on my last twizzler. I continued to critique my competition as I watched from the bleachers. *She shouldn't be jumping left; she should be spinning right!* **What is this?**

I fought back my disappointment as I saw this group screwing up Mrs. Smith's dance routine. The group before them was on point! No doubt about it; I'm sure they're going to be first in line.

That bothers me, but at the same time, there is always a second in line, right? "Klaus, your group is up!" Ms. Smith yelled as she grabbed her iPod. I ran to the front of the group as Finn slapped my back.

"We're gonna do this, and we're gonna do this right." I just smiled and nodded my head. We were the best dance group in Louisiana. Not even Mrs. Smith could tell us otherwise.

"So, how is it?" My mom asked me with such enthusiasm in her voice. I took one more bite and savored the delicious taste.

"Amazing as always momma," I replied while stuffing my face with more cornbread and mac-and-cheese, you know, *soul food.*

"Do you have dance practice tomorrow?" I looked at my mom with a; *you already know we made the team*, look. As spontaneous as she was, she smiled and proceeded to talk. "Don't get too cocky, but you're right."

I nodded my head and bit into my cornbread as I took my compliments. "How's your lucky mark doing?" My mom asked, as her eyes looked down at my wrist.

"Good, mom, it's doing good," I said, as I itched my wrist under the table.

"Any lucky numbers come in yet, like lotto numbers or something?" My mom asked me, as she gave me a smirk.

"Not by a long shot, mama. I'm telling you, mom, there's nothing special about me." My mom shook her head. I hated lying to her. But she would never believe me if I told her what I could do or if I told her what I had been doing.

I looked up from my plate and smiled to avoid suspicion. "You have never been wrong, mama," I replied with a mouth full of cornbread. As I did that, she just burst into laughter. I shook my head and laughed along. Everything was going to be okay. As long as I kept my mouth shut, and as long as I kept my power under control.

Ok yeah, I can't sleep! I thought to myself, as I began to get up. I kept having this dream about this girl. Not that I have my eyes fixed on anyone, but this was different. This girl was in… I think outer space or something. Then a huge asteroid plummeted to earth!

Sure enough, the girl ends up right in *my* dance audition. *Honestly, I've heard of "before-the-first-day chills" or whatever, but this… this is too much.* It was… it was so weird. I could feel her pain, I could feel her fear, and it was like I was *there*. It was like I was… *her*. I rolled out of bed and walked slowly to the bathroom.

As I began to turn on the light switch, this sound rushed passed my ear. I stood in front of the mirror as I saw a figure behind me. The sound screeched, "Can anyone hear me!" My body began to get goosebumps. I felt a harsh chill against my neck. I ran out of the bathroom as fast as my legs could carry me. I'm *sure* I left my shadow behind.

I was long gone by the time I heard the bathroom door slam behind me. I stumbled and scrambled for the doorknob in my dark bedroom. I turned on the lights in my room and sat on my bed. Thoughts began to race in my head. *Was it the dream that was bothering me so much? Am I really THAT nervous? Who was the girl in my dream?* My thoughts filled my head more and more by the second.

It got to the point where my head started to pound. "AHHH!" I screamed at the top of the lungs. I slid off my bed and onto the floor as I clenched my head in pure agony, blood coming from my nose, eyes, and ears.

The girl's scream filled Klaus's head, as it got louder and louder. Before he knew it, he felt a hard, painful impact to his head, causing him to slam on the floor. He began to bang his head on his bedroom dresser uncontrollably. It was all over. He couldn't feel anything. Klaus was gone.

So, there he lay, passed out, blood slowly dripping from his cold ears onto the white floor tiles of the now deadly silent room.

Chapter Four

Davina and Octavia rode the bus in silence. Until that is, Octavia broke the silence. "What does the house look like?"

Davina raised an eyebrow and turned her head to Octavia and began to speak as expected. "*Defiantly*, nothing special, if that's the response you were looking for," Davina replied, slouching lower in her seat.

"Ok, then…" Octavia began to get out of her seat.

"Wait, I'm sorry" Davina apologized, as her hand was tightly squeezing Octavia's arm. "It's fine. It's fine." Octavia sat back down and gave Davina a big grin, as she prepared herself for more questions. Davina didn't smile back though, which surprisingly didn't bother Octavia.

Octavia began. "What's your…"

I'm not answering that!" Davina yelled, shocking even herself as she turned heads of some of the people around her. "Nothing about family Octavia."

Octavia looked down in embarrassment. "I understand, sorry, that was stupid of me."

Davina nodded her head quickly. "Yeah, it really was." Davina anxiously replied with a small grin on her face. Octavia slowly analyzed Davina in amazement.

Davina looked completely different when she smiled. It was almost scary if you think about it, with her baked complexion along with her light gray eyes and just a few freckles on her nose, forehead, and cheeks. Then with her puffy orange hair, she was something to admire. You don't come across many biracial kids who look like this, around here at least. But Davina was who she was, so it was what it was.

The bus started to come to a halt. People began to get up, as the bus driver called out. "Next stop, up ahead!" Octavia and I proceeded to get off the bus. As we did, I threw a thumbs-up to the bus driver. He did same back. Then he slammed his bus doors as he drove off into oblivion.

I turned to Octavia, in an attempt to carry a good, not *too* rude, conversation. I had to; she needed to know the rules of foster care, and who knows, maybe I'm one hell of a teacher?

"Which house?" Octavia asked in utter horror.

I calmly understood exactly why. "Yeah, this house isn't the best." Octavia still stood in shock. "*Really*, not at its best." I made that remark as subtly as I could, but I'm pretty sure Octavia was going to need a lot more than rules to survive this household.

"Aye, snap out of it Barbie, it's not like-*that* bad." Octavia did just as I said. She started to walk to the house as I placed myself directly behind her.

Knock, knock. Octavia knocked on the door and waited for an answer. As we stood there, I felt Octavia glance at my wrist. I quickly pulled my sleeve over my birthmark to avoid any other questions.

Octavia just smirked as she continued looking at the door. "New tattoo, huh?"

I looked at Octavia and smiled. "Wow, how did you know?" I asked her while holding back the truth.

"I saw you scratching it on the bus; maybe it's infected, you might wanna get it checked out or something."

I shook my head. "I'll be fine, and you will too," I whispered to Octavia in a different tone than what I had been talking to her in. "I'll explain everything once we walk inside, okay?"

She just nodded her head slowly. Looking at her facial expression made me pity her. I sometimes forget that this is a reality and day-by-day, new kids enter this system and leave their *non-eligible* families.

The door finally opened. This **buff**, grumpy looking white woman flung open the door. "Huh, isn't there supposed to be an escort or something?" Octavia sternly spoke, surprising the heck out of me.

"Well, My apologies, but she dropped me off at the school, and yes, I don't think she was supposed to do that." I nodded my head. I had to admit I was impressed. She shifted moods pretty fast, good for her.

"May I come in?" Octavia asked, as she poked her head in and began to analyze her new home. I noticed she was surprised to see three other kids with three different nationalities and three *very* different personalities. As I began to walk in, Ginger eyeballed me and gave me the "introduce me" eye motion.

So, I began. "Octavia, meet the gremlins." As soon as the words left my mouth, a sharp pain pricked my butt. "OWCH!" The others laughed as I calmed myself down. I gestured as if I was introducing royalty, going gremlin by gremlin. "This is Ginger." I gestured to a little girl with hair like mine. But she was Caucasian and had *lots* of freckles.

"They call me sticky fingers," she squeaked with a smug grin. Octavia reached out to shake her hand. I quickly stopped her.

"If you like that ring on your finger, you won't shake her hand," I whispered into Octavia's ear, as she calmly pulled her hand away.

"High five?" Octavia offered, as Ginger studied her hand. Ginger didn't budge. "Okie Dokie, then." Octavia sighed, as I walked her down the line of her new housemates.

"This is Prishna." Prishna looked a bit older than us as she smiled and waved at us. She was South Asian, and Octavia seemed to be in a trance by her long, silky, black hair as it ran down her shoulders.

"If you're wondering, they call me Stiry Curry. I cook tasty food, but I can also make someone sick if I wanted to." As Prishna said these words, I just smirked and slowly looked at Octavia because, hey, it was so incredibly true. She just smiled and winked at Prishna, as if to say, "Cool, don't poison me, thanks!"

"Curry wouldn't hurt." Prishna giggled, as she gave Octavia her nickname recommendation. Octavia cheerfully nodded as I continued to show Octavia, the *bunch*.

"This is Gerard Dung-Hai." He looked up at me with a strange look as I said his name. "Come on man, why the whole thing?" He rolled his eyes at Octavia, and their eyes met.

"I'm the typical Asian nerd, nice to meet you." Gerard bowed and reached out his hand for Octavia to shake. Octavia smiled and shook his hand.

She leaned back and whispered in my ear, "He seems really nice."

I unnoticeably pulled her away as I explained my thoughts to her. I just shook my head. "Yeah, he seems nice now, but just wait till you touch one of his computers; he'll go straight out Korean on you." Octavia rolled her eyes before I could stop her, she walked over to Gerard and started a conversation.

I managed to slip away from the crowd. I walked to my room, intending to leave Octavia out there to chat and become familiar with the gremlins. Not long after I had entered the room, I started to get bored.

I took out the quarter from my pocket and twirled it in the air, controlling it with my mind and hand motions, slowly moving the quarterback and forth. After playing with my unique skill for five minutes, I bent over and opened my backpack in search for my journal. I grabbed it out of my backpack and kicked my bag under the bed.

I plopped back on the bed, looking at my journal. I started to read what I wrote earlier that morning. Suddenly, things got blurry. My heart started to pump, and soon after that I began to zone out again - *it's happening*.

My eyes rolled back as blood started dripping from my ears. I whipped out my pen and started stabbing words onto the paper as my hands shook. *I'm finishing this*. I began to see the scene right in front of me, my head throbbing with memories.

September 20, Nine years back

I saw these black, thick, entities flying out of his mouth as he screamed in pure agony. Blood began to stream from his hollow eyes and mouth. I was numb. I couldn't run away. I couldn't call for help. I couldn't cry. I just stood there, as I watched my father die.

So, there I was. My father was on the floor, bled out. My mother was in the next room in the same state. And there was me, traumatized, stuck in the same position he left me in: standing numb, unable to move, bloody arm, and beyond terrified.

The only difference was, as I started to analyze and understand what had just happened, I was able to cry. Tears began streaming down my face. Soon after, I saw a spider-like creature in the corner of my eye.

My eyes got bigger and bigger, as it quickly sped toward me. I screamed as loud as I could as I struggled to move. It leaped forward, three inches away from my face. I didn't stop screaming. As soon as I thought my life ended, I heard the front door open.

The creature vanished faster than I could recognize the door had opened. A small, young Hispanic woman began to open the door to my room. She yelled and began to cry hysterically as she grabbed me and shook me.

I assumed she saw the knife in my hand and assumed *I* did all of this. But sure enough, she saw my traumatized face and analyzed the scene and probably concluded that I did this out of self-defense and that my mother was dead first before my father.

She held me in her arms as she sobbed and analyzed the scene with me. "What did you do?" I was in a trance as she asked me a thousand questions. She began to call 911. She was a neighbor; I think my parents knew her well. Because she was telling the cops **everything,** she knew about the Michaelson family.

The police came, startled by the scene. The woman turned to me and grabbed my hand. I calmly let her take me to the kitchen. But as we passed it, I snapped and began to cry. I noticed my mom's eyes blink right in front of my eyes.

I yelled and screamed. "MOMMY!" I pushed the woman and began to run to my mom. One of the policemen picked me up. I hollered. "Get up, Mommy, it's okay now, we can leave!"

I bit the officer and struggled out of his grip. I quickly ran to her and shook her. *Mommy, get up,* I thought in my head as one of the detectives slowly tried to grab me.

My mom's eyes were opened, but her eyes were hollow. Suddenly, one of the detectives grabbed me and carried me out of the living room area. I turned around and lifted my hand.

As I opened my fist, a pan from the kitchen came out of *nowhere* and hit the detective in the head. Another officer picked me up before I could use my ability on him.

I kicked and yelled. "She's alive! You don't understand! She's not dead!" I cried loudly as the officer that I bit took me and injected me with a yellow liquid. Everything went blurry.

I took one last gaze at the horrifying scene: my father bloody on the floor, my mother's eyes opened but not blinking in a puddle of her own blood. I dropped to the floor. The Hispanic woman picked me up and carried me to the cop car. That's the last time I ever remember seeing my parents. Well, in human form at least.

Chapter Five

Klaus lay in a room that was filled with familiar faces. His eyes opened slowly as Finn ran up to his face in disbelief. "No way, he's awake," Finn exclaimed in utter shock, as Klaus's brother, Merfie, peered into his eyes.

Klaus was surprised to see Merfie, but he was in even more shock when he saw that he was in a hospital bed. Klaus began to sit up as he felt his head. Finn and Merfie began to back away.

"What… what happened." Klaus noticed his mother was asleep, and so were Finn's parents.

"I don't know. You tell me, bro," Finn answered back as if Klaus was some type of psychopath. Klaus flashed him a confused look and turned to Merfie, who was rubbing his hand on his forehead stressfully. Finn began to speak with a scared look on his face. "Klaus… why did you try to kill yourself last night?"

I tried to analyze the words he just said but, I couldn't because was so surprised, so I forced out a short giggle under my breath. "What the hell, Klaus? What's going on with you?!" Merfie firmly asked me as I felt my face. "The doctor said you bashed your head against a hard surface until you went unconscious, his estimate was seven or eight times."

I slowly looked at Finn when he said that. He finished. "And the doctor said it was on *purpose*."

I began to speak, confused as ever. "All I remember is running into my room after a really weird experience… then…then…" I couldn't finish because I couldn't remember what happened after I ran into my room, after hearing and seeing something out of the ordinary.

This girl… *Did I fall asleep? And why couldn't I reverse time…none of this makes sense;* I thought to myself as Finn and Merfie studied me.

"Then what?" Merfie exclaimed.

"I don't know…" I answered in a trance.

Finn shook his head and leaped at me in relief. "Thank god you're alive, man!"

Merfie chimed in. "Yeah, we thought you were dead."

I raised my left eyebrow and shook my head. "Why?"

Merfie looked down to the ground and muttered: "You lost like, *a lot* of blood when we found you."

I looked at Merfie in curiosity as Finn studied my heartbeat on the hospital monitor. "We?" I asked with a hint of surprise in my voice.

"I mean, we heard your screams from the room." Merfie continued. "Finn was just at the door with me, we were planning on surprising you with my appearance since I've been gone for three years."

"And what makes you think I would be happy to see you…" I questioned Merfie, as Finn quietly observed. Merfie slowly nodded his head, so I knew he understood. "Listen, alright I just want to know why the heck people think I tried to kill myself, and how I supposedly **bashed my head in** repeatedly, and somehow I don't remember any of this."

My brother, Merfie, walked towards my bed and put his hand firmly on my shoulders. He smacked his lips and began to speak in a charismatic tone. "You should know that you are getting more stitches than the ones you already have." He quickly let go before I could attempt to punch him with my weak arms.

Finn began to shake, as he tapped the monitor. "Klaus… where is your heartbeat?"

I quickly turned to the monitor. I had no pulse. According to the monitor, I was pronounced dead 12 minutes ago.

Chapter Six

Mazikeen had been sitting on the floor for an hour, and still, nothing had happened. She got up from the floor and shook off her uneasy feeling. Mazikeen walked over to the heater and popped in some space burgers while watching home videos.

To her surprise, for the time being, things were as normal as they could get. She played the first tape. It was back when everybody was on the space station, and everything seemed ok. Mazikeen watched as the tape rewound to the better times.

Times when she was who she was when she was happy. "Come on, Maze!" Her father shouted as he smiled holding her hand. Mazikeen's thoughts raced as she remembered where this was. It was in their condo on the 4th floor of the space station. It was Christmas morning, and it didn't take

Mazikeen long to notice that. The Christmas tree and her big sister caught her eye.

"Mazie! Open it!" Mazikeen's little brother screeched as he jumped up and down. Mazikeen's big sister continued to sleep under the Christmas tree. Mazikeen grabbed her brother and bit his cheek. Don't ask; it was a phase. Her younger brother, Abdul, hollered as their mother picked him up and kissed him on the forehead. With Abdul's cheek printed with Mazikeen's bite, her father began to laugh.

"It's not funny, Marcellus!" Her mother hissed, as Mazikeen began to laugh too. Mazikeen smiled. For the first time in 12 days, she actually smiled. Tears began to flow from Mazikeen's eyes as she watched the videos. She quickly wiped them and shut the camera off. She couldn't bear the feeling she felt when she came to the realization that her family is dead, hundreds of families are dead, that she's trapped in space, the fact that she's still alive.

Even worse, she'll probably never get an explanation why. Mazikeen plopped her head on the pillow next to her and let her dreams save her from this traumatic nightmare.

I couldn't sleep. I closed my eyes for 30 minutes, but I wasn't dreaming. Suddenly, I heard a slow long creaking noise as If a door was slowly opening. *What's that sound?* I thought to myself as I got up from the couch. I peered my head around the corner of the game room entrance, as I caught a glance of what seemed to be a bulky black figure. I was about done with all these *surprise* visitors by now. *Out of the hundreds of people that died in the space station, who could this one be?* I thought to myself, as I approached the spot where the figure had stood a couple seconds ago. I waited for the fear bottled up inside me to burst out. I felt a soft touch on my face. I quickly stumbled back, landing on what seemed to be a piece of broken glass. I began to study my leg. Blood began to make its way down my leg. *"CRAP!"* I angrily huffed as I attempted to get up.

No luck, and no use in trying. I couldn't feel my left leg, and I didn't need the puddle of blood beneath me to tell me how bad my situation was. My mind began to race, as the red puddle didn't just grab my attention, it stole it. *Ok...* I began to think. *Everybody suffocated, meaning there's no oxygen left in the space station. I learned in my science class that blood is blue or purple inside the body. My blood is bright red right now.* I stopped dead in my thoughts as I began to process this. "No Way…" I began to feel queasy. *No… freaking… way…* I took a deep breath in and out.

I couldn't believe the words that shot out of my lips next. "I'm…I'm breathing air." I felt a soft touch again, as I got dizzier and dizzier. The puddle of blood under me kept getting deeper and deeper. "I'm actually breathing air…" I mumbled under my breath as I went unconscious.

Chapter Seven

"Davina." Ginger shook Davina as she began to wake up. "Davina get up; it's time for dinner, and why is their blood on your bed?" Ginger scrunched up her nose. "Is it that time of the month again?" Ginger asked, as Davina lifted her head off her pillow and slowly began to rub her eyes. Ginger sat down next to her. "Are you alright?"

Davina just nodded her head and ruffled Ginger's hair. "Yeah, I'm fine."

Ginger wrinkled her nose and kicked Davina in her side. *"Hey, little brat, watch it!"* Ginger sped out of the room as Davina chased her. Davina was finally gaining on her when a firm voice halted them in their tracks.

"No running in this house!" Ms. Marth growled. Both Davina and Ginger rolled their eyes.

Ginger stopped running and slowly turned around "I'd beat you if I joined track." Ginger exclaimed while quickly flicking Davina off.

Davina smiled and shook her head. Davina ran over and squeezed Ginger's fingers to teach her a lesson. Ginger quickly let go, squealing. It was always fun when Davina played with Ginger, the love they had for each other was strong.

"Ginger, go help Ms. Marth in the kitchen," Davina ordered. Ginger stuck her tongue out at Davina and did what she was told. On that note, Davina looked for Octavia. She walked through the unkempt house and wondered where Octavia could be. She suddenly remembered that she was talking to Gerard. She remembered that she told Octavia to not go anywhere without her. Yet Octavia still managed to slip past her. But still, that wasn't going to stop Davina from knowing Octavia's whereabouts. So, Davina followed the path to his room as the darkness of the hallway consumed her.

I finally reached my destination as I stood in front of Gerard's door. I heard laughing and excessive mumbling, as I reached for the door knob. I slowly leaned in and peeked through the opening crack of the door, so I could ease drop on their conversation. I barely knew this girl, so it couldn't hurt to know a little more about her, right? What can I say? I like to learn. I pressed my ear against the door and listened in on their conversation. "Yeah, I know right! That's just crazy!" Gerard seemed to be agreeing with Octavia, as I heard her laugh.

"Yeah, I see them sometimes, even in my dreams." I couldn't believe what I was hearing. What does she mean by *they appear to me in my dreams?* I began to lean in deeper so I could hear. This conversation was getting too good just to walk away.

"Are you serious?"

"That's cool, Octavia. I wish my parents could do that," Gerard replied in a sentimental tone. There was a long silence. Then I finally heard a serious sharp voice bounce off the door and pierce my eardrums.

"No, you don't." Curiosity got the best of me. I slowly began to open the door even further, just a little, just enough to see what was going on. The door made a light screeching noise, but they didn't seem to hear it. I guess they were too involved in their conversation to notice. The voice sounded like Octavia's, but it was way too deep and eerie for me to sort out.

"Are you… are you okay, Octavia?" Gerard asked while slowly reaching his hand out to place on her shoulder. I saw them sitting on his bed, facing each other, but not *too* close. Either way, I didn't know Octavia was so open with strangers.

Ok, stop thinking random thoughts, focus, Davina! I thought to myself, as I continued to watch the scene unfold.

"I'm fine. I'm alright." Octavia finally responded as she held the pillow in her arms. "What they do to me in my dreams, the messages they show me, the stuff they make me do…"

Gerard pulled her in for a hug. I was so confused, and wondered why is she letting him touch her? They just met two hours ago. For crying out loud, we haven't even had dinner yet, and he's already making her his main course.

I began to think to myself. *Why is he so nice? Why didn't she talk to **me** about this in-*

stead of him? I thought we had a complex friend-ship going! I thought we could be - I stopped myself. The word *Best friend* hasn't left my mouth since I was five. I don't do the whole "friend" thing. Honestly, it's too time-consuming. I'm better off on my own.

"For the last time, it's time for dinner. Get to this table *now*!"

Oh no. I knew that voice. It was Ms. Marth's pissed off voice. That was her "you're gonna get everyone's scraps if you don't run like hell to this dinner table voice."

Apparently, my legs knew that voice, too, because they gave up on me as soon as I began to run to the kitchen table. Instead of getting up, I fumbled and banged my head on Gerrard's bedroom door, flinging the door wide open and blowing my cover – worse than I thought was possible, by the way.

The look Gerard gave me was a million words jumbled all into one. *Really?* My face was flat on the floor. I slowly got up from the floor and cracked my neck. Octavia looked like she was about to burst out laughing. I quickly dusted myself off. I cleared my throat and spoke as I gestured to the opened door. "You are all wanted at the dinner table."

They both gave me the strangest look and casually approached the door. I cheerfully moved out of their way and suspiciously followed behind them, awaiting the delicious meal I smelt dancing around my nostrils. *I see now what Octavia's going through. I had gone through the same thing before the incident happened with my parents*, I thought to myself as I entered the dining room and sat in my seat.

"This is going to be one interesting dinner conversation," I muttered under my breath, as I stared down Gerard and Octavia. But you know what? I'm sure they can say the *same* thing. I'm <u>certain</u> of that.

Chapter Eight

Finn began to press buttons. You could just see the panic in his eyes. Merfie had to calm him down by holding him back. "Don't touch anything, you idiot!"

"Are you a doctor?" Klaus screamed as Finn tried to break free from Merfie's grip. Don't think Klaus was calm because he wasn't. A sickening feeling filled his stomach as he looked over to his parents. *How are they still asleep?* Klaus thought to himself.

Merfie ran to their father in distress. "Wake up, Dad, wake up NOW!" Faster than any of us expected, a doctor sped into the room. She paced over to the monitor. Merfie's father, *Mr. Alvarez*, began to wake up. His eyes shook rapidly as he realized Merfie was waking him up.

"Oh, it's just you." Mr. Alvarez exhaled in relief as he began to sit up in his chair.

"Dad," Merfie whispered, trying not to wake up the rest of the family. "Something's not right with Klaus."

"Ouch! That hurts…" I exclaimed as the nurse drew blood from my left arm. They had an IV hooked to my right arm, but I had no idea why. A woman in blue was checking my monitor, as my family and friends sat and stood calmly watching them, and worst of all, me. I was a bit embarrassed that they thought I was suicidal. But what really confused me was how I didn't remember any of it. Nothing! Not a clue and that girl's face was still etched into my memory.

"It's missing," the doctor muttered under her breath while squatting down looking at the wires. I turned my head to look at what she was talking about. She slowly walked up to me and extended out her hand. Her soft green eyes caught my attention. As she stood above me, I fought back a smirk growing on my face.

"Where is the cord, love?" As she asked me, her eyes glanced down at my wrist. She quickly picked up my arm and studied my birthmark with her index finger. "Aren't you a little too young to have a tattoo?"

My mother sat up in her chair and responded, "Doctor, it's his special birthmark." The Doctor looked at me in approval as I nodded my head. I lay there mesmerized by her eyes, hesitant to speak. But even so, she still hadn't answered the question.

I didn't get what this woman wanted from me. I managed to gather up the strength to speak up. "Um, what cord, what are you talking about?"

She then kneeled beside my bed and began checking underneath my body. Her hands were as cold as ice. I squirmed in confusion and discomfort. Suddenly, she stopped. She got up and stood near my feet. She then began to search over where my feet were.

I felt a tug around my ankles, as the doctor unraveled this long gray cord from underneath my left ankle. It ended around my thigh. I couldn't believe what I was seeing. *I had the cord all along!*

"But how is this even possible doctor," my father said, as he jumped up to defend my case. "Klaus can't even get up on his own, let alone get off the bed and unplug a complex device." *This isn't normal,* I thought to myself, as Finn gave me a look of disbelief.

"How… even…" Finn mumbled under his breath.

"Help me," I mouthed to Finn.

He nodded slowly as he mouthed back, "I got this."

You see, Finn and I have a dance future ahead of us. This whole incident is going to mess that up BIG time. Even though Finn was hysterical, Finn knows that deep inside I would NEVER try to kill myself. I bet Finn was just as confused as I was when he found out the head injuries were intentional. *What's happening to me? Maybe I really am going insane.*

"So, you mean to tell me you didn't know you had the cord."

I was silent. The doctor shook her head and looked away. Five minutes and some awkward silence went by, and still, I heard murmuring going on amongst the other doctors in the room.

"I honestly had no idea it was in this bed; I didn't even feel it." The words flew out of my mouth so quickly that I didn't even real-ize I had said them. But they were true.

The nurse checked the chart as Finn left the room. Just as quickly as Finn left the room, a tall, well-built black man of my same color squeezed into the room. I sat up in my bed as my mother slowly approached me. Tears filled her eyes as she rubbed my forehead.

"I'm just glad you're okay, Klaus." I placed my hand on top of my mother's hand as she spoke those kind words to me. I knew what was coming next. I could see it in her eyes.

"Hello, my name is Mr. Halleck." He extended his hand. "Nice to meet you." He introduced himself as my mother shook his hand. Soon after that, I shook his hand as well. Slowly, but I managed.

"There aren't any beds open here, but I managed to find some at another backer act facility two hours from here." The man said, calmly flipping through his pages.

Are you kidding me! I thought as I looked around for Finn. *No way, they're just going to assume that I'm suicidal?*

"Mr. Halleck will try to contact any closer locations," the doctor added.

Mr. Halleck continued, "But ma'am, beds close up quickly."

One of the nurses reassured my mom.

"Dinner is on its way, so just rest and we will take care of your son, Mrs. Koster," Mr. Halleck pitifully said, as he patted his clipboard against his leg and made his way out of the room. He gave me a warm glance, then continued making his way out of the room, pulling shut the glass door behind him.

Chapter Nine

Mazikeen slowly opened her eyes and began to blink rapidly. She tried to move but she couldn't. She noticed that she was in the infirmary in the space station, six floors higher than where she originally was. She tried to get up slowly, but the unbearable pain of her leg pushed her right back down.

She began to study her body as she flexed her arms. There was a note attached to her big toe as if she was dead. Mazikeen thought to herself, *so they think they're funny, huh?*

Mazikeen slowly got up and stretched her hands to get the note from her big toe, fighting through the pain. She stretched and stretched as she felt her leg cramping up. Finally, she managed to reach the note, as her back slammed back down with a firm *thud*.

She slowly lifted the note to her face and began to read every scribbled word. Her eyes began to widen as the note wrinkled in her hand. *Oh no…* Mazikeen thought to herself. She let out a scream so loud I'm pretty sure the demons could hear her. The thing is, that's *exactly* what they want.

I have to get out of here!" I struggled to get up, but a force was pushing me back down. "Let me go, dammit!" I yelled as the force pushed me back down again. I started to panic as I screamed in utter terror.

A bulky black figure was slowly approaching me. *This was different! This couldn't be a ghost. This thing is too evil! What is this?*

I knew I couldn't just lay there and die, so you know what I did next? I put up a fight. I rolled off the table onto the hard, cold floor. I hustled with my arms and elbows over to the door, as the black figure got closer and closer. I finally managed to get out of the room.

I quickly strained to slam the door behind me as the figure rapidly banged against the door with all its force. I closed my eyes and focused on my current situation.

Then I began to hear voices. I concentrated even harder, as blood began to drip from my ears. Finally, I could make out what was being said. ***"Take her life, so she won't meet the others!"***

I quickly snapped out of it. My birthmark began to itch and sting. *They're trying to kill me!* I thought in a panic as I looked down the hall. I squinted my eyes and saw an open door. As I thought of rolling down there, the door behind me suddenly stopped banging. *Huh…* I thought to myself.

I no longer felt vicious vibrations from the other side of the door. Instead, I felt an ice-cold sensation down my spine. Faster than lightning, I jumped away from the door and onto my side. "Ughh, why the hell is this thing torturing me?" I muttered under my breath, as one side of my face was now smushed against the cold floor.

Out of the corner of my eye, I saw a tall, black figure speeding up to me. I began to pray in my head. I quickly raised my head and started rolling faster and faster by the second, sucking up the pain, letting my will to live to be my strength.

As I was rolling down the hallway toward the opened door, I noticed a head pop out from the corner, a blurry white head. I halted in my tracks and quickly turned my head back to see if the other figure was following me. The figure was just standing there.

Then when I snapped my neck back around to see if the white figure was still visible, I quickly noticed that there was a black figure behind the white figure, and the black figure was … it appeared the black figure was strangling it!

The whole spaceship started to shake as if we were falling out of space. All the red emergency lights and the loud beeping made it clear. We were falling out of space. I started screaming as I glanced over at the open door. Right at that moment, the door slammed shut.

*There **must** be another way. It just can't end like this. I just can't die like this. I'm still alive for a reason; I have a purpose.* I rolled to the elevator as fast as I could. As I entered, it was full of blocks of ice. Regardless, I climbed in and pushed the button to close the door.

My blood began to mix with the ice, and so the ice began to melt rapidly. The elevator dropped suddenly, and it felt like I was levitating as the cursed machine plummeted down to the last floor of the space station faster than could blink. I was scared and afraid. The cold was an understatement; I was freezing.

The elevator suddenly came to a complete stop, which stopped the hovering, so I slammed to the elevator floor into my own blood with a loud *clunk*.

The elevator door slowly began to open as the water spilled out of it, tinting the white floors with a light red. I struggled to stand on my feet, but it was no use; I had lost too much blood.

Suddenly, the room I was in burst into flames. *The space station must be getting closer to earth.* A cold tear slowly made its way down my cheek. I was going to die.

I began to sob loudly, drowning out the sound of the harsh flames. I found myself huddled in a corner looking at a red button as I quickly wiped tears from my eyes.

I squinted my eyes and made out the words: *Emergency drop.* THAT'S IT! I rolled through the flames as fast as I could into this small maxi glass tank. "Why hadn't I ever seen this before?" I said to myself, as I closed the tank door. Right in front of my eyes was a logo. I wiped the ash from the logo to read it clearly. *Norwood Creations*. My eyes grew big; I couldn't believe what I was seeing. I began to scoot back in confusion. "Dad?"

As I said my deceased father's name, my back hit the red button. I became detached from the space station that very second. I looked up and saw another blurry white figure. "NOO! DAD! WHY IS THIS HAPPENING? PLEASE, PLEASE TELL ME!"

It looked exactly like my father, and he was waving goodbye to me. Just like that, every memory I had of him, my family, myself… was gone.

Chapter Ten

The family began to gather at the dinner table, as Davina followed behind the mysterious duo. Davina pulled out a chair and placed her napkin on her lap. She glared at Gerard and Octavia. *This is gonna be interesting*, Davina thought, as she began to dig into her bourbon chicken.

"Can you please pass the mashed potatoes?" Prishna asked as she scarfed down some sausage. The juices began to run down to her chin as I passed her what she asked for. As usual, I was multitasking. As I handed my fellow pupils food, I watched Gerard and Octavia on the side. I was so focused on them that I forgot to be my usual spontaneous self at the dinner table.

"Umm, Davina?" I quickly snapped out of it and turned my head to Ginger.

"Are you alright?" Ginger asked as if I had five heads growing out of my left elbow. So dramatic, I swear.

"Yeah, yeah, yeah, I'm fine, why?" I replied as I continued scarfing mashed potatoes down my throat.

"Hey, slow down, or you'll choke!" Mr. Marth hissed.

"Yeah, Davina, jeez..." Gerard chuckled with a sarcastic smirk on his face.

My thoughts were racing. So fast, too fast! I couldn't even swallow. I wanted to know what Octavia's parents made her do, and what images they showed her! I slowly swallowed my food and prepared to speak.

Prishna studied Octavia. "Where are you from?" she asked.

Octavia looked up from her plate and smiled. "Oh, um, I'm from Louisiana. I was born here."

Prishna raised her eyebrows, smiled, and nodded her head before she went back to eating her chicken. Ginger tapped her fork on her plate in utter boredom. I couldn't wait any longer.

"So, do you have any..."

I began to cut Gerard off. "Octavia!" I exclaimed.

"Yes, Davina," Octavia answered with a smile on her face.

"So I … So, I heard something" I started to come clean in a shaky voice. Octavia's smile disappeared from her face, and a look of worry spread across her lips.

"What…" Octavia hesitated, as she forced the words out of her mouth. "What did you hear?" Octavia muttered under her breath as her eyes began to turn watery.

I took a deep breath and placed my fork on the table. I slowly picked my head up and locked eyes with Octavia. "What happened to your parents?" I demanded.

Her face began to turn red as a tear fell down her cheek.

"Davina, chill, alright!" Gerard snapped while slamming his hand on the table. Everyone froze, even Ms. Marth.

"It isn't a pretty story." Octavia strained to say through her tears.

Prishna stood up. "Look around, love, do any of us look like we have pretty stories?" Prishna gave Octavia a sympathetic look.

Octavia began to speak, but Gerard interrupted. "Listen, you don't have to share this if you're not comfortable."

Ginger slowly turned her head and clenched her fist. "Gerard, if you don't shut up and let this girl talk, I swear to God."

Everybody's eyes widened in hysterical shock and looked at Ginger.

"Don't use his name in vain, dang," I muttered as I slumped down in my chair.

Finally, Octavia began to speak. Everyone slowly moved in closer to the center of the table to hear what she had to say. As they did, Octavia started her story.

"My parents, they… they… died." We didn't look the least bit moved or surprised, so she continued. "But the way they died, they… their eyes were-"

My heart raced, and my mouth spat out the word, "Hollow."

Octavia's head quickly turned to me, as our eyes locked. Octavia's expression was scary. A look of terror crept onto her face. "How the hell did you know that?"

My eyes began to water, but I promise you not a *tear* fell. "Because my parents died too, and it was more than hollow eyes, Octavia, so tell me what you think it was," I said with a look of despair on my face. Deep down inside, I knew what killed her parents. I just wanted to hear her say it. So, I know I do not imagine things, so I know I'm not crazy.

Octavia slowly tilted her head down and whispered the name. I couldn't hear her; I doubt anyone could. A silence waved over us as I got the courage to ask. "What did you say?"

Octavia looked me dead in the eyes. "I killed them, but what I killed wasn't them." I looked away from her glance in shock.

"It was the darkness inside of them that attacked me. Before they attacked me, three blurry black figures watched me sleep that night, then the next morning my parents were found dead in a pool of their own blood."

Prishna covered her mouth in shock. Tears began to fall from her eyes, Gerard's eyes widened, and terror could be seen on his face.

Octavia continued: "I woke up scared and wanted to run to their room for help, but by the time I got there, the demons had already killed them…but…"

Octavia stopped and looked at her hand. I was confused. *I thought **she** killed her parents*, I thought to myself.

I tapped the table with my fork as Octavia continued speaking. "I was horrified, I slowly bent down to touch my mother's pale, cold face, when suddenly she woke up.

Actually, both my mom and dad slowly got up with smiles on their faces as if they were happy to see me." Octavia began to cry. "But at that moment, I noticed something wasn't right. Their eyes were hollow, and the sockets were bleeding.

"It looked as if they were crying tears of blood. Then my mother stood up, she grabbed my neck, and my father began to pull my hair and chant some type of demonic chant." Octavia wiped the tears from her eyes and kept going. "I feared for my life, but also for theirs."

"I remembered where they kept their *special* gun, so I kicked my mom off me and succeeded in getting my dad to let go of my hair. I scrambled for the gun under their bed as my knees scraped against the rough carpet. I finally had it in my hand as they mounted me."

Ginger left the room in tears. I understood why. I don't know why I didn't tell Ginger to leave the room sooner. I felt terrible seeing Ginger so broken by a story that I forced out of Octavia. But I had to stay, even though I already knew how this story was gonna end. But I guess Octavia knew that I knew because what she said next, still until this day, never leaves my mind.

"I couldn't believe I was about to kill my parents, but the thing was, they were already dead, so what attacked me that day wasn't my parents, they were demons. I rolled over and shot them both in the head. I was 11 at the time, and I… and I know that I didn't kill my parents!"

Octavia fell to the floor and began to ball her eyes out. "They died long before I could have possibly ended their lives!"

Gerard tried to pick up Octavia, but she wouldn't budge. She was glued, crying on that floor, and I presumed she wasn't going to get up without finishing what she had to say. So- she continued.

"The cops came, and they asked me what happened. I told them through tears that they were fighting and I heard two gunshots, and I ran to see what happened, but by the time I got there, they were both dead.

"The black figures took them from me!" Octavia hollered.

My head started to ache. This was too familiar to me. I've seen this before, I've heard this before, and I've *experienced* this before. Our stories were so similar, yet so different and there was no doubt that it was abnormal what happened to our parents. My thoughts suddenly stopped racing. I squinted my eyes. I couldn't believe what I was seeing. In fact, *was* I even seeing this?

It appeared that behind Octavia's head a black hand was slowly creeping out of the shadows behind her.

"You say the black shadows took your parents away from you?" Ginger asked in her sweet, innocent voice.

"I know they did,," Octavia said, as she held tightly onto her arms.

I began to feel weaker and weaker. Octavia slowly turned her head in my direction, the black figure still right behind her.

"Because I see them right now," I muttered before hitting my head on the dining room table, knocking me unconscious.

Chapter Eleven

Light began to shine in Klaus's eyes. He quickly pulled the sheets over his face again. But the bright lights still shined through.

"Get up, time for breakfast!" A buff man informed as he beat against the opened door. Klaus got up from his bed and sized his roommates. *I still can't believe this*, he thought to himself, as he climbed out of bed. He sat on the edge of his bed, put on his hospital socks, and walked out of the room.

As he crossed the other rooms, he noticed all types of atmospheres. He slowly began to walk up to the breakfast table, as several of the girls in the room eyed him closely. He quietly took his food and sat alone at the table in a big, green plastic chair.

He softly placed his forehead in the palms of his hands and tried to recap all that had happened less than eleven hours ago.

It was dark, it was cold, and it was silent. Everyone in the hospital room was sleep, except for Klaus, who was wide-awake. Suddenly, three hard knocks echoed from outside the door. It was Halleck.

"Come in," Klaus groaned in a raspy voice, as Mr. Halleck began to step inside the room. He studied Klaus as he lay in bed, completely unbothered by his presence. "Did you get any sleep at all?"

Klaus slowly shook his head, still tucked away under the covers. Mr. Halleck looked up as he turned on the room light. "Ughh!" Klaus grumbled in agony, as the bright lights pierced his eyes. Apparently, the excruciating pain of the lights had the same effect on everybody else because Mr. Halleck heard the same reactions all around the room.

I was tired of this; I just hoped the place I was going to has Wi-Fi and some good food at this point. My mother stood from her resting spot and slowly got up to shake Mr. Halleck's hand.

"Yes, I found a room for your son, Mrs. Koster." Mr. Halleck explained. "His transportation is ready to load him."

Wow, I thought to myself as I rubbed my sore, stitched-up head. *This is happening, huh? I'm just going to go to this random place, just like that.* I peeked my eyes out from under the covers to glance over to Merfie. He was sound asleep, snoring as if he meant it. I looked around for Finn. I saw him, literally on the edge of my bed, near my feet, drool and all, sound asleep.

"Just bring him out in the wheelchair when you're ready." Mr. Halleck answered as he exited the room.

My mother walked over to my bed and slid under the covers with me, tightening me in her grasp. Her cold, damp, shaking body filled my warm, fuzzy covers as I too began to shake from her cold body temperature.

"Mom, are… are you ok?" I whispered under my breath so only she could hear me.

She pressed her left cheek against mine and answered back in a heartbeat. "I love you, Klaus. If you're okay, I'm okay sweetheart." Her tender, warm words made me feel like everything was gonna be okay. But I knew it wasn't going to be.

As I lay there, slowly drifting back to sleep, I noticed a shadow approaching me from the right side of the hospital bed. I couldn't make it out at first. I thought it was Merfie. No, no it couldn't be him, not a chance. *Hold on. Wait.* I thought to myself, as I lay there paralyzed with fear and the weight of my sleeping mother. *That's not a human.* My thoughts raced as I attempted to get up from the bed.

The figure slowly began to approach my face. I honestly thought I was going to wet myself. Suddenly, I heard a deep, awakening voice from the bottom of my bedside. "Hey Klaus, you mind not trying to bash *my* head in?" Finn exclaimed as he rubbed his head. I guess while I was trying to scoot away from the odd entity, I harmed Finn in the process.

It is sure as hell looked like it because Finn moved to the chair where Merfie was to continue his slumber. I just sat there, dumbfounded by what had just taken place. Before I even had a second to think, I heard two firm knocks on the glass door. It must be Mr. Halleck telling us *Klaus aut to be on his way.* My mother sat up in the hospital bed with tears filling her big, brown eyes. She was wide-awake and filled with anguish… I could feel it.

"Alright, are you ready?" Mr. Halleck asked, holding my clothes in an odd tinfoil bag. I was only permitted to have my hospital gown on for some odd reason. But at least I had an orange blanket they put over me when I entered the ambulance. My mom was by my side, along with my dad and my Best friend, Merfie.

It was time. It was time for my dreams to be crushed into a million pieces and for me to share those feelings with crazy people in an unknown building. My father rolled me in the wheelchair down the colorful, peaceful hospital hallways. As he pushed me, we quickly approached a huge black van.

A lady sat in the driver seat with rows and rows of chairs behind her. This was it. *Am I really going huh?* I thought to myself, as I felt hugs begin to attack me.

"HANG IN THERE, MY DUDE!" Finn screeched, as he hugged my back then punched my arm. Merfie just beat on my chest and wished me good luck. That was expected. I wouldn't expect anything more. If he tried to hug me, I don't even think I would have let him.

"Are you ready to load him, Mrs. Koster?" The Women driving the van asked softly.

I looked up at my mom and gave her an *I'll be just fine* type of smile. She hugged me lightly and bent down to kiss my forehead, leaving a red kiss smudge on me. Then she kissed my wrist. "Your lucky birthmark will keep you safe, trust your instincts." I looked up, and I saw determination and love in my mother's eyes. I nodded my head and smiled back.

Finn and my dad helped me out of my wheelchair and slowly placed me in one of the seats in the van. When I entered it, I automatically wondered what type of children sat here before me. As I thought this, my friends and family stood by the door, as Mr. Halleck slammed the van door shut and reassured my family that I'd be ok while escorting them back into the hospital.

Chapter Twelve

Friday 12, 7:12pm

Can she stop staring at me…? I thought to myself, as I noticed the woman driving this van had a fixed stare on me through the small van mirror. I began to look at my surroundings. This van must have carried about 18 people at a time. I heard a voice suddenly arise from the awkward silence; It was the van driver.

"Are those contacts son, because if so, you'll have to remove them?" She asked me confidently.

"No, no ma'am this is my real eye color."

She shook her head in disbelief. I slowly nodded my head. "That's just fascinating," she firmly replied. In response to her reply, I turned my head to the window, raised my eyebrows, and chewed on my tongue. It was always a habit of mine. The van bounced up and down, causing me to grow an excruciating headache.

About 15 minutes passed by when I noticed that this van had **no seat belts**. *Wow, I* thought. *These people are taking us to a foreign unit, and they want to kill us before we can even get there? Yeah, before we can do the job ourselves.* I shook my head and attempted to fall asleep. With this shaky van, it would be a miracle. *Hmm, or maybe it's a "safety hazard."* I thought to myself as I placed my head on the hard leather seats.

I was just about to doze off to sleep, but something caught my eye in the seat ahead of me. *Was there another kid on the van? What? No way! I'm the only one on here. Wait…* My thoughts began to take over as my body became damp. I had a bad feeling. My wrist started to shake and itch. *That thing… that, that figure; I've seen it before!*

I sprang out of my seat and moved to the other side of the van, curling up my legs onto my chest. My pupils widened as my eyes became watery. An awful pain filled my chest. I began to gag as I fell to the dirty floor. Blood began to pour out of my nose. I glanced over to the driver; she didn't notice I was in pain.

"Ma'am, please, help me, I… I can't breathe, please." I managed to force those words out of my mouth when suddenly I heard a loud piercing scream. I saw the *same* shadowy figure wrapped around the driver attempting to enter her mouth. I went into shock. "WHAT THE HELL IS GOING ON?" I hollered at the top of my lungs. I looked out the window to see if any passengers in cars are just as freaked out as I am by seeing what's going on in this van. I looked back at the driver and… and I'm absolutely confused. I rubbed my eyes and looked at her again. I blinked my eyes rapidly. She's perfectly fine.

I felt a pressing sensation on my hands. I looked down at my hands and saw a blue mist begin to surround my fingertips before making its way around my wrist. My birthmark began to glow a light blue. I looked up to see the van driver groaning in pain, coughing and hacking.

Klaus Koster! *Klaus Koster!* An eerie screech filled our ears. I tucked my head in my hands and covered my ears. The voice continued for three minutes; this was pure *agony*. Then it just stopped.

"You're one of the demons?" I uncovered my ears and slowly looked up. The driver was giving me this mortified look as if I was the entity. She simply radioed someone as she fixed her hat. I sat there terrified. I finally knew why I was here and why all of this was happening. I'm being followed by a demon, and its goal is to take me.

Chapter Thirteen

Klaus took his head out of his palms and shook his head. Flashbacks always made him dizzy, but never like this. He got up to get some breakfast from the front desk. Two girls examined him and smiled when he selected his breakfast choice.

He grabbed his food and slowly made it back to the green plastic chair where he had been sitting. When he arrived, he dusted off the chair and began to eat his food calmly. *What am I doing here?* He thought to himself. *Why is this thing after me?* The flashback from back in the hospital contaminated his brain. The flashback didn't answer all his questions. But he just had the feeling this couldn't be good. So, like any sane person, he feared for his life.

I was almost done with my food, and I was on my way to throw out my trash until a girl stopped me in my tracks. She had long, light brown braids in her hair and freckles all over her face. She was directly in *my* face. At that point, I slowly backed up, but I was still at a conversational distance. I mean I couldn't just walk away.

"Do you need anything?" I asked as I placed my palm on the back of my neck in uneasiness. She just discarded the fact that she was two inches away from my face and began talking.

"Did you hear about all of the commotions last night?" I raised my eyebrow and looked around in confusion. "There was a huge explosion! All the staff and workers went out there, and they claim they found a half-naked girl out there covered in blood!"

I slowly nodded my head. I know I'm "insane," but did I really have to associate with the insane? I just wanted to be left alone at this point. But judging by the glares from the guys, and the long awkward stares from the girls, my wish certainly wouldn't be my command.

We stood there in silence as she studied my eyes. I then mustered up the strength to ask a question. "Um, exactly how did you get all this information?"

A soft smirk crawled on the girl's face as she replied. "Well, we go outside like twice a day, so when it's time to go outside, when all of the staff is on break or not looking, I sneak into the computer room and look at their files to see if we have any new people coming in this place."

I nodded my head in agreement. *"Nice,"* I exclaimed while silently applauding her bravery. To be completely honest, I was proud of her. I mean, how did she get away with all this? I looked down at the ground then back at her face. She seemed chill.

As I began to study her, she continued. "And that's not all, I watched the footage of last night, and I'm pretty freaked out about this."

I began to walk away to go sit on my green plastic chair, and I motioned to her to sit with me. As she walked over, I noticed a symbol on her neck. Oddly, it kind of looked like the symbol on my wrist. My instincts were tingling. But I chose to ignore it. *Could she be... like me?* I thought as I averted my eyes away from her neck.

"So, what do you think is gonna happen to her?" I asked, as my leg vibrated due to my ADHD.

She just shook her head in doubt. "I really don't know." I leaned back in my chair. She was pretty to me, but there's always a story with everyone.

"What's your name?" I asked her, as I fidgeted in my seat. "Aaminah, that's my name." Aaminah looked off into the distance as she answered me. It wasn't long before she spun her head around and asked for mine.

"It's Klaus." What she said next made me go numb.

"It's spelled clause but Pronounced as Klaus. It can go both ways; it doesn't matter." I slowly turned to her with a confused look on my face.

"You know everything, don't you?" Aaminah just rolled her eyes and nodded her head. I looked at her and smiled. The expression on her face started to change as she stared at my lips. I also noticed that I could feel that the air inside was getting hotter.

"I'll be right back okay?" At that, I got up and went over to one of the staff members at the desk. I looked back at Aaminah, and she gave me a smirk.

I looked at the ground as I approached the front desk. "Yes, young man." As I Looked up, a woman was there filling out papers. "Um, how long am I going to be here?" She looked up at what she was doing and answered.

"Honey, as long as you need to. You tried to take your own life, that's serious. I hope you know that?" I let out a huge sigh and put both of my hands on my face. "Thank you, ma'am," I responded back as I shuffled back to my seat. "My pleasure sweet pea."

I sat down at one of the tables and put my head down. I drifted into a tired state as I fell asleep beside Aaminah.

Chapter Fourteen

Smoke filled the air, as Mazikeen lay there, covered in her own blood, unconscious in the same tank from the space station. She struck the earth with a huge **BANG.** Her heartbeat was just as rapid as the blood gushing out of her foot, but she still managed to survive.

She attempted to look around, but there was a thick mass of gray smoke blocking her vision. All the stuff Mazikeen knew about earth was from a tape they showed her when she was 11 years old. From her knowledge, she was in the year 1975. Back in the space station, the station leaders would show them sketches of the earth.

People taken in, smuggled pictures up onto the space station even though they were told not to. The story behind man kind's existence in space was a blur to Mazikeen. All she could recall from past stories was that a man by the name of Arthur Fremantle saw the world ending in one of his dreams in 1923.

He was suspected to have lived in the time era 3045. The most interesting part was, he was also suspected of having supernatural abilities to teleport into any era he wanted. So, after his dream, he went back into the 1900's to save as many people as he could with the space station his great Grandchildren had created. So, Arthur crashed a hot flapper party in New York and took thousands of people up with him.

That's really all the information she had. They informed every one of the current era earth would be in, and from Mazikeen's remembrance, it was definitely the 70's. She had spent her entire life in space. Not once had she ever dreamed that she would be on earth. But the previously impossible had, become a reality. So now, it was up to her to find out the past; it was up to her to find out the truth.

It was dark, and I was cold and afraid. I started coughing from the suffocating smoke that filled the air. I looked up, and I felt like I wanted to faint. I saw stars... I *saw* stars. I tried to stretch my hand to touch them, but the pain from my leg dragged my hand right down. I slowly crawled out of the space tank and dug my hands into the damp, soft dirt.

I began to cry out of happiness as my fingernails became filled with mud and tiny leaves. My hands began to shake as I felt the cold, sharp blades of grass. My fingertips moved all along the ground as I savored this amazing moment. I couldn't believe it; I was on earth. I was sitting on grass- breathing natural fresh air. I fought through the pain as I began to pull grass from the dirt. With my last bits of strength, I huffed and puffed as I rolled over on my stomach so I could attempt to get up. My palms were bloody, and my head was pounding so hard I couldn't even feel the cold air on my skin, numbing my body.

I managed to sit on my rear as I noticed these bright lights approaching me. A tall, buff man approached me. More and more cars approached, along with people in even *bigger* cars with these contraptions in their hands that they were holding up to their mouths as they spoke.

The man picked me up and tightened me in his grip. I yelled in pain. "Ouch!" I began to thump on his chest. "Let me go!" He acted as If I didn't say I word, and he kept on walking to the entrance up ahead.

I was running out of options. I pulled my head back and bashed it against his skull. He screeched as he dropped me. "AHH!" I hollered as my leg slammed against the hard ground. I quickly got up and attempted to run. As I did, lights flashed in my eyes and people were taking, it appeared photos of *me* with nicer and more modern looking cameras. I was limping to nowhere as the freezing, wet air began to consume me. Tiny cold drops of water began to fall from the sky, wetting everyone in its path.

I began to get dizzy, and everything started to turn black all around me. My cute dress at this point was ripped up, burnt, wet, and covered in sweat and blood. I couldn't bear this pain much longer. My vision failed me as I dropped to the ground like a rag doll. My head pounded as I went unconscious. I had arrived. But I never imagined it would be like this. I never thought I would be so stuck and so alone… but I was. I was.

I opened my eyes to see white above me.

It seemed to be a bright light. I squinted my eyes as two women hovered over me. The woman on my left pulled the light away from my face as the woman on my right held a clipboard. The woman with the clipboard whispered into the other woman's ear and walked out the door. "Where am I?" I managed to push the words out of my sore, dry throat.

The woman turned her head in my direction and softly replied. "In a safe place, darling, in a backer act facility."

As I took in these words, I noticed something. There were these white pieces of what seemed to be hard cloth around my left leg. All the blood was cleaned from my body, and all my cuts had been treated. I attempted to lift my leg, but the woman stopped me.

"Now, you want to rest alright, take it easy."

As those words came out of the woman's mouth, I studied her forehead. I slowly nodded my head. I looked at her name tag, and it read *Nurse Nancy.* I looked down and began to think. *So, these women are nurses...*

I pondered on that. *Do they know where I had come from? Do they have a place for me to stay? Can I just leave and handle this on my own?*

Tears started to fall down my face as my cheeks became hot and red. The nurse quickly looked down at me. I realized I was showing weakness, so I quickly wiped the tears from my face.

The nurse looked away and smiled. "You know dear; it's okay to feel pain." I rolled my eyes and nodded my head in response. "Trust me, I would know," she answered back, as she was unraveling a brown box covered in yellow stickers.

And so, would I, I thought back in my head. The nurse handed me some huge baggy clothes. I held what she gave me firmly to my chest. The nurse pointed to a room.

"In a day or two, you will be told to go through those doors to get checked into the Backer Act unit." Nurse Nancy looked at me as if she expected a response back.

I blinked. I wasn't about to stay in this room isolated for two days; I had to meet other people and learn more about this planet. I couldn't just stay here. I couldn't just lay here and do nothing. My leg hurt so much, but I had to make up something, *anything* to leave.

I squeezed my fist together. I shook my head rapidly and began to speak. "I'm fine, nothing hurts. I have a white wrapping around my wound, and the nurse said it was just a scratch, so I should be fine."

Nurse Nancy looked me deep in the eyes. "Go to that room, and a woman in all tan will be right with you shortly."

I processed what she just told me. "*Go to that room.*" Can I even stand up? Let alone walk to a room that is on the other side of this building? I slowly closed my eyes and began to think. *I want to meet people from this planet, but I can barely walk. I better just stay here for a day or two as the nurse said.*

I opened my eyes and looked at the nurse. I guess she felt my glare and she peeked over her shoulder and smiled at me. I gave her a dead look. I still don't know why I didn't just smile back.

Chapter Fifteen

avina lifted her head up from the cold, floor tiles. She looked around. It was dark and foggy. Everything was pitch black. Her ears were ringing, and she could smell what seemed to be gas. As she slowly got up, she felt a cold liquid on her feet. She bent down to touch it as her body shook in fear.

As she bent down to touch it, her fingers became numb. Davina didn't know what was going on. In fact, this started to ring a bell in her head, as if she had experienced this event before. Davina touched her face as she felt a hot sensation on her cheek.

Suddenly a burning sensation slapped her in the face before she could even realize what hit her. She automatically fell back bumping her arm on the table. "Hello! Is anyone there?" Davina cried out.

She covered her face and breathed heavily through her mouth for fresh air. Davina lifted her arms and attempted to use her ability to throw the chair with her mind into the window in front of her. But it was no use; she was too weak. Davina heard a rumbling sound coming from behind her.

She slowly turned her head in fear. She didn't want to turn around because she knew what she was going to see. Now she remembered the smell, the darkness, and the fog before the demons took her parents. The thing that took away her parents was about to take her too.

I couldn't move. I was paralyzed with fear as I slowly turned my head.

"Davina, Davina it's me… it's me, Octavia." A faint, rough whisper came from behind me.

"Octavia?" I whispered back, as I got up with all my remaining strength.

"What the hell is happening?" Octavia spoke in a frantic soft voice. Regardless of how calm I tried to act, I was terrified. If what I thought was *actually* happening, we wouldn't make it out alive.

Octavia shook her head rapidly, as she looked at me and began to speak.

"I can't find the others," she continued. "I think we're not safe here, I smell gas, so I'm guessing if we don't find the others and leave soon we're going to be blown to bits."

I stood paralyzed as I was taking in all this information. To my knowledge, we were screwed either way. All this made no sense to me. I couldn't imagine anything bad happening to the others. But deep down, sadly I knew it was a possibility. But I couldn't tell Octavia that. I won't tell Octavia that.

I turned to Octavia and took a deep breath. I felt like her eyes were staring deep into my soul as I opened my mouth to address her.

"Look, Octavia – we need to go call for help instead of sitting here like fresh meat."

Octavia's eyes widened, and her lip began to tremble.

"W... Why would you say that?" Her breathing got heavier as I attempted to calm her down. But she only continued to panic. "Fresh meat, why… what is coming for us?"

I grabbed her hand and yanked her in my direction.

"Okay, Octavia, I understand you're upset right now, but we need to get out of here and find help."

We ran down the hallway and flung the door open, slamming it behind us as we ran out of the house barefoot. As we were approaching the middle of the street, Octavia pulled her hand away from my tight grip. She pushed my chest and attempted to do it again.

Before she could even try, I blocked her hit and held her hands tight. She squirmed and squirmed, but she couldn't get herself free from my grasp. Face to face, we were looking at each other, out of breath with our hands tied up in a pretzel.

Breathing heavily, Octavia finally spoke.

"What did you mean by fresh meat dammit!" I just put my head down and pressed my lips together. I untangled from her grip and rubbed my wrist to get rid of the pain. I couldn't believe how strong Octavia was for a girl with such skinny arms. After about five seconds of silence, I was ready to respond.

"Octavia… I know what happened to your parents."

After I had said that, Octavia's wide eyes grew narrow, then she looked at me with an angered look in her eye. Her eyes began to wonder as she clenched her fist.

"Did Gerard tell you that?" She looked away, and tears began to flow down her red puffy cheeks.

I shook my head.

"I was listening to your conversation when you told him; I was behind the door and… and I heard everything."

We just stood there in the middle of the abandoned street, contemplating our next move. I turned my head to my shoulders; I heard something. It sounded like a crying child. I turned around.

"GINGER!" As soon as I saw her, I dashed to her side.

"Davina, what are you doing?" Octavia ran after me. "Why are you running to an empty road!" Octavia hollered after me as she slowed down her running. "Where are you running to?" Octavia hollered in confusion.

I approached Ginger, and I held her in my arms. As I did that, she stopped crying. Ginger slowly looked up at me. As she looked at me, I froze with terror in my eyes. Who I saw was not Ginger. Her eyes were hollow, and she smiled a huge, disturbing smile at me. My heart began to beat out of control as I began to understand what I was holding in my arms. It wasn't Ginger; it wasn't even human.

"DAVINA WATCH OUT!" I heard Octavia holler from down the street. I looked in her direction. As I did, out of the corner of my eye, I saw lights that looked like they belonged to a car. I turned my head back toward Ginger in my arms. But to my surprise, my arms were empty.

I looked up, and before I could get out of the street, a huge truck struck me and cleared me from the road. Octavia ran to me and shook my bloody body. The last thing I remember was her stunned, afraid face as she cried over my body. Her face was the last thing I saw before my body shut down and I went unconscious.

Chapter Sixteen

Klaus felt a tingling sensation on his back as he began to wake up from his nap. He raised his head to find Aaminah poking at his back. He plopped his head back down and covered his face with his arms.

"Hmm, Aaminah let me sleep." Klaus groaned as he shook his shoulders. He couldn't get what happened in the van out of his head. He turned his head to look up at Aaminah.

That symbol. Klaus thought. *What could it possibly mean?* Aaminah noticed him looking out of the corner of her eye. She turned her head and looked at Klaus. He quickly turned away, as his cheeks turned bright red. Aaminah smiled and shook her head.

"Hey, you, curly top." Some tall looking blonde boy called out to me.

I turned my head in his direction and smiled.

"Aye, wuss good?" I was used to being called *some sort* of name based on my hairstyle by now, so I had no need to fight the guy. Plus, pounding his face it would probably get me more days here anyway, so why even bother? Honestly.

The boy reached for the box of crayons in the middle of the table and started drawing.

"The names Calvin, Calvin Cline," the blonde boy said while coloring the elephant on the paper *ever so neatly*.

I nodded my head in understanding but paused.

"Wait, you mean *Calvin Klein,* as in the clothing brand?" Calvin shook his head. "No, Calvin **Cline**, not **Klein**," he continued. "But everyone just calls me Cline."

We all stared at him. Then finally I broke the silence. "Aye, that's neat." I reached over the table to *Dap handshake* the kid and grabbed some crayons and a sheet of paper for myself. I noticed him analyzing me, so I colored slowly, thinking of my every move.

Aaminah took some crayons from me and started sketching on the table. Calvin broke crayon after crayon as he attempted to draw what looked like a cup of "grape juice" on his paper next to the elephant he was previously coloring. I looked over at him, and he caught my glance. He looked down at his paper and resumed coloring.

"How did you get in here, Curly Top?" I looked up once again, rolling my eyes as I gave Calvin a side smile.

"My name's Klaus."

Calvin began to laugh. "Oh noooo, okay, okay, one of the C's I see."

I shook my head.

"It's spelled with a K." I smiled at Aaminah because she knew it wasn't.

Calvin paused and looked up at the ceiling with his eyes squeezed together as if he was solving the hardest math problem you could ever think of. After three seconds of comical silence, Calvin just scoffed under his breath. He mouthed the word *bastard* and rolled his eyes. The whole table noticed, and before I knew it, my ears were ringing with intense laughter. I just shook my head.

Aaminah suddenly broke the sound that was music to Calvin's ears.

"Answer his question, Klaus," she said sternly, as the small group of kids at our table all glanced over at her.

I puffed up my lips, scrunched my forehead, and shook my head in confusion.

"What question?"

Aaminah just gave me *the look.* You know that look that your parents give you when you ask a stupid question? Yeah, that look.

Honestly, they aren't going to understand nor believe me when I tell them, but what can I do, right? So, I responded, but with hesitation in my voice.

"I'm not suicidal." I looked down then up again.

Calvin just looked at me like I just said I was an illusion. Calvin sat back in his chair as if he was butter on hot toast. He began to speak as the rest of the table intensely listened.

"You're not suicidal, huh?" He mumbled under his breath.

Then he spoke up.

"Curly Top, neither am I, but I'm still in this hell hole," Calvin continued. "Klaus, Klaus tell me *how* you got in here."

Aaminah looked at me with a hard-looking face. She mouthed the words "Go on."

I took notice at all the faces paying attention to me. They wanted a story, so they were gonna get one. One way or another, everyone would know my story. Everyone would know what happened to me; it's only a matter of time; it's *always* just a matter of time. I kind of wanted to hear everybody else's stories too, so it's only fair if I tell mine. So, I started.

"I was at my house like normal, and I was trying to get some sleep, and…" I looked at Aaminah. She nodded in approval, so I went on. "I couldn't, for some reason, I couldn't get this girl out of my head. It was like I could feel her pain and I could see what she was seeing. It was like I was her… in a way, you know."

Calvin nodded his head in understanding, but his face showed fear and confusion. I knew deep down that they all thought I was crazy as hell. But I had no other choice but to keep on talking. I started again as I scratched the paper around my purple crayon.

I decided I needed to cool down in my bathroom, so I walked over and attempted to splash some cold water on my face. As I did, I heard this blood-curdling scream right next to my ear, so I quickly picked up my head, and then when I looked in the mirror,

I saw this weird blurry figure behind me and the bathroom had turned freezing cold. I ran out of the bathroom, and all I remember is jumping onto my bed and slamming the door shut.

I sat on my bed and rubbed my eyes, and that's all I can remember. The next time I opened my eyes, my head was pounding, and I was in a hospital bed, hearing doctors, friends, and family all telling me that I tried to kill myself. I was shocked. This all makes no sense to me."

The table was silent, *dead* silent. I looked over to Calvin. His pupils looked dilated, and his face looked pale, like the paper he was drawing on. I looked over at Aaminah. Her eyes were wide and watery. Then out of nowhere, I heard one of the kids at the other table snicker to himself.

"Haha, damn this kid must take more spice than I do."

Calvin turned his head sharply in the boy's direction.

"Shut up with ya Afro Jack looking ah."

The boy just laughed and shook his head. He replied, "Cline, are u serious?" The boy jumped up from his seat and rubbed his hands together. "Bruhh, that's why you're built like the cinnamon stick that runs around with the apple." As soon as that was stated, everyone at both tables looked at Calvin then burst out laughing." I was shock too. He *really* tried Calvin man I can't even lie about that.

Calvin gave him the middle finger with a neutral face. Surprisingly that's all he did.

"You straight, man? I see things too. Anyway, here's my story." He began to clear his throat.

"Hold up; you're serious?" I leaned in, as Calvin did same.

"Of course, of course. After I take a hit, I experience all types of things, my man."

My face dropped, and I leaned back in my seat. I couldn't believe it. They think I was high when I "Tried to commit suicide." *Unbelievable,* I thought to myself, as I huffed out a frustrated breath. I looked over at Aaminah. Her face looked flushed, and her hand was on her neck, covering where the symbol was.

"I have to go use the bathroom, excuse me." Aaminah slowly got up and walked to the bathroom, as she continued to cover the symbol on her neck. We watched as she faded into the darkness.

"Aye, Curly Top, you ready?" Calvin snapped in my face like he was some type of magician and his objective was to break me out of a trance. I snapped out of it.

"Yeah, yeah, yeah, I'm good. I'm straight."

Calvin gave me that *look*.

"You sure, Curly Top?"

I looked at him and laughed. "Yeah, I'm fine, tell your story already."

Calvin smile quickly faded, and his movement became slow. "Alright, so it all started when I was at my step dads house. Well, it was my mom's house, but my stepdad paid all the bills, so he called it *his house*." Calvin continued. "I was sitting in my room playing video games. It was my cousin's Xbox, so I was super careful with it because he let me finesse it for the weekend. So, I heard my mom and my stepdad fighting, and you know, I never really liked my step dad."

Calvin stopped and looked me straight in the face. "You ever owned a gun before, Curly Top?"

I shook my head quickly.

"Nah, man, that's one step closer to getting put out on the streets."

There was a pause. So, I justified myself.

"My mom always tells me that."

Calvin shook his head. I looked over at Calvin with a straight face. I guess he got the idea, because, he continued his story.

"I knew how my stepdad could get with my mom, so I took out this gun my friend gave me for protection, tucked it in my pants, and headed outside to see what was going on.

"I walk outside to see him on top of my mom beating her face in, and I just couldn't take it anymore… I flipped.

"So, I sped to my stepdad and pushed him off her. I pushed my stepdad to the wall, and I put the gun to his head. I told him if he hit my mom one more time, I would blow his brains out."

Calvin turned and looked at me.

"You see, Curly Top, that was a stupid idea considering this man was twice my size."

I nodded my head and Calvin continued.

"So, after my *not so smart* move, my stepdad pushed me to the ground and started knocking the snot out of me. He tried to take the gun out of my hands, and his finger went on the trigger and then…" Calvin looked down, and his face began to turn red. *Oh man,* I thought. I felt a bad feeling in my stomach as I saw tears begin to fall down Calvin's face. "You see these tears, Klaus? I hate crying in front of people."

I moved closer to him and rubbed his shoulder. I felt his pain. Calvin attempted to continue through the anguish.

"My stepdad and I were fighting for the gun, and I don't know what happened. The next thing I know, I heard a loud noise, and I see my mother's forehead covered in blood and her pink nightdress stained with red, and she just fell to the floor."

Calvin shook his head and wiped his tears.

"I killed my mom, Klaus… I… *killed* her."

I took in all that I was hearing, but things still didn't add up.

"I'm so sorry that you had to go through that, Calvin, but exactly how did you end up here?"

Calvin raised his head, and with a straight face, he wiped the last tear that was making its way down his cheek. Then he began to speak.

"I… I saw what I had done, and all I could do was freak out. I saw my mom just bleeding out on the ground, and I just went into shock. I couldn't imagine a life without my mother because she was the only family that I had. So, I got the gun and pointed it to my stepdad and pulled the trigger." My face dropped, and I think Calvin noticed, as he looked down and went on.

"I missed though, so I just decided to off myself, so I put the gun to my head like this,"

Calvin demonstrated by making his hands into a gun. He put the imaginary gun to his head and pulled the trigger, but nothing happened.

"I ran out of bullets, Curly Top." He began to laugh quietly as he spoke. "I ran out of freakin bullets, so I tried again and again to push the trigger, but nothing happened.

"My stepdad noticed what he had done, and he called the police saying that I tried to kill myself and that I had also killed my mom in the process. "I was so deep in shock that I fought the cops when they came to take me, and they had to inject me with this thing that calms you down, you know, booty juice, the stuff they give us here when we act up."

I nodded my head, but I had no idea what he was talking about. Truth be told, I could care less what *booty juice* was because I know for sure I won't be getting any anytime soon. I could see Calvin in the corner of my eye dosing off. I gently shook him, "Finish." I asked quietly. He nodded his head and continued with his story.

"So, in two weeks when I get out of here, I'll probably be facing court and going to jail for the death of my mom. I don't even know at this point."

Calvin rubbed his forehead and put his head down on the table.

"We'll get through this together, Calvin," I replied as I shook his head playfully.

Calvin smiled and answered back,

"But we just met, ain't no way you care about me like that."

I shook my head.

"Don't be stupid, man I'm here for you, so you better start getting used to it."

It's been a while since I've seen Aaminah. I wonder why she's in the bathroom for so long. I patted

Calvin's back and got up to stretch my legs. Then I began to walk down the hallway. As I was walking, I heard a grumpy, concerned voice ask me a question. "Where are you going, young man?" A woman dressed in all green asked me as she fixed up the food for lunch.

"I am going to the bathroom ma'am."

She nodded.

"Alright, go along."

I smiled at the woman and kept on walking down the hallway. I heard odd whispers. Like what I was hearing wasn't English. As I approached the bathrooms, it got clearer and clearer. Suddenly, the girl's bathroom door slightly opened. I peeked through the small opening. I saw a shadow on the wall, but nobody was there for that shadow to belong to anyone.

I felt chills run down my back and up my shoulders. Before I could react, the door silently closed, as If someone was holding the doorknob and then gently closed the door. I quickly stepped back from the door. *Aaminah was in there, but I didn't see her.* I swallowed my fear and went to the bathroom. After what I just saw, I **needed** to go.

Chapter Seventeen

I finished doing my business and started to head back to the table where Calvin was. To my surprise, everyone was already seated and eating their lunch. I couldn't believe my eyes. The food looked decent. Scratch that, the food looked amazing! You would think since this place is for troubled teens they would feed us like troubled teens, but this place was extremely clean and cozy for what it was. *Wow, I might have to come here for a bite instead of Wendys*, I jokingly thought, as I pulled up a chair next to Calvin. *Wait a minute.* I looked around and noticed that Aaminah wasn't anywhere to be found. *That's weird.* I turned around to find Aaminah sitting on one of the plastic chairs. Relieved, I motioned to her to come over. I picked a tray, and I began to pray, as she pulled up a chair. As I was praying, I felt eyes on me. I wrapped up my prayer and looked up. **Everyone** was staring at me. I slowly opened my carry out the box and started eating my fries. I tried to ignore the observing eyes that I could see out of the corner of my eye.

"OOO RIGHT!" Calvin spoke up as he attempted to swallow a mouth full. "Let's say grace." Calvin extended out his hands for the people near him to hold. The girl on his right did same, but the guy on his left just sat there and side-eyed his welcoming hand. Then I heard a voice from behind me. "Just take his hand, Bishop, you got nothing else to lose." Nurse Nancy hollered.

The boy to Calvin's left, Bishop, took his hand and let out a deep breath. "Now, let's say our grace." Calvin bowed his head, but only five kids did same, as they recited several prayers. I was taken a back; I didn't know that Calvin knew how to pray, let alone spit out Bible verses and know prayers that were used in my kindergarten class.

"Alright, let's eat!" Calvin ended his prayer and started to devour his plate faster than any of the others. A girl stood up and walked over to Calvin and hugged him from the back. She smiled and shook her head. "Your impressive, Calvin, join me for Bible study sometime."

The girl laughed and made her way back to her seat. She looked extremely attractive. Like… *very* attractive. Like Aaminah level attractive. The girl's beautiful dark skin and bouncy curls were beyond attractive.

"Yeah, you know how it is, for you I'm nothing but spontaneous." Calvin turned to me and grinned. "You see, Curly Top, that's how you do it." I paused. "Using the bible to get religious girls." I laughed and held my stomach. Calvin noticed my focus on my wrist and grabbed my arm. "Man, Klaus, you got an infected tattoo or something?"

I quickly grabbed my hand back. "Nah, this is my birthmark. It itches every now and then but it's nothing serious." Calvin shook his head. "No, Klaus, that seems like something serious look at it, it's turning blue." I quickly raised my wrist close to my face. *It was turning blue.* I put away my wrist and changed the subject. I was too scared to think about my birthmark because I feared this mark on my body wasn't **just** a birthmark.

The thought of that made it hard to breathe. "Anyway, what were you saying before?" I exclaimed as I sat up in my chair. "Oh right, I was saying how you have no game, Curly Top." *Is he talking to me*? I thought to myself as I kept looking behind me. "Klaus I'm… I'm talking to you, buddy."

I couldn't help myself. I busted out in laughter. "My guy, have you seen me?" I shook my head and cracked my knuckles. Calvin nodded and swallowed his last bit of fried chicken, while his bacon remained swimming in a pool of fries. "You might have the looks, Klaus, but you ain't got no game." He motioned over to the other table. "You see Ebony or Amanda or whatever her name is all the way over there?"

"It's Aaminah" I cut in. "Well she moved away like ten minutes ago to go sleep at the other table, and you didn't even notice."

Calvin was right; I didn't notice. I smirked and slid my back into my chair and folded my arms. I shrugged. "Okay, so what, I'm not that great with girls, whatever." Calvin looked over at me and laughed under his breath before he drank his mango Snapple. Calvin kissed his teeth as he turned the cap

back on the Snapple bottle. "Go talk to her."
"She's not my type," I answered back.

"Now you know that's a damn lie, Klaus." Calvin continued to speak up. "I'm gonna go shower, alright. By the time I come back, you better have her number, address, and social security number." I bowed my head and smiled. *Man,* I thought as I giggled to myself.

"You so damn goofy," Calvin said, laughing as he slapped my back. "Alright, I'll be back in a little bit." We Dapped before he walked away. He looked back and motioned to me to go to Aaminah. I nodded my head and got up. I had more important things to worry about, but Aaminah seemed like she had something to do with what I was worried about. I just had to figure it out. As I made my way over there, a short Latin-looking girl stopped me in my tracks. She had some nice eyes. I just stood there frozen as she began to talk. "I can help you."

I raised my eyebrow. "With what…" I said in fear. *Did she know? Did she know what I was going through? Her? Nooo. Not for a second. I mean why would she know, unless… unless she was like me.* All these thoughts were rushing through my head, as I stood there stiff as a statue. *What could she be talking about…* "I can help you with Aaminah. I can see you're obviously into her, she has been here a while; I can help." The girl cut me off in my train of thought.

My head suddenly relaxed. "With Aaminah? What makes you think I need help?" I asked hesitantly. Why are random people getting into my business at a time like this? She looked up at me with her shiny, brown eyes, which wasn't helping. I looked back down at her. "What's your name?" I questioned her, as I stepped up to her. "Not your concern." She stepped back as she smiled. "Okay, *not your concern*, I don't need your help." I looked back for Calvin then continued talking. "But thank you for the offer." I walked away and felt the girl's eyes piercing through my back. I got to Aaminah. She looked my way and smiled. "It really took you *all that time* just to come and talk to me?" Aaminah said with a smirk on her face. "What are you, eight years of age?"

She tied her black boots as she zipped up her black jacket. She jumped up from the chair and folded her arms in front of me. Without realizing it, I began to concentrate on her eyes. My eyes followed down to her neck. I had a weird feeling in my chest. I remembered my mom telling me to trust my instincts. I had a thought of putting my symbol to hers and seeing what would happen.

The moment that thought crossed my mind, Aaminah's smile slowly faded from her face, her eyes began to water, and her pupils grew large. She blinked after five seconds and slowly shook her head. She looked uneasy. But she just shook it off and smiled. I could tell something was up. I looked back down at her neck. "Hey, Klaus, I'm up here." Aaminah desperately tried to avert my eyes from her neck. I snapped out of it and shook my head. "Yeah, sorry." Aaminah looked tired as she stood in front of me. Drained would be a better description. *Did she sleep at all since she arrived here?* I thought. I rubbed my head, thinking of what to say next. She caught on and continued. "Let's go outside, Klaus. It's almost time to go for our evening outside break, let's just go ahead. They won't mind."

I stepped in front of Aaminah blocking path. "They won't *mind,* or they won't *notice*?" Aaminah smirked, ready to be her witty. "I think you know which one I mean, Klaus." With that said, we snuck out into the outside area and sat on the piercing hard benches. I glanced over at the closed bolted gate and the green grass on the other side.

"Have you ever thought of escaping? You know, just being free." Aaminah looked at me; then she shook her head. "No, I haven't. Have you?" She turned to me and asked. "No, I haven't, because I – just got here," I responded as I threw little rocks into a cup. I faced Aaminah as I placed the rest of the rocks I had on the bench. "Aaminah… why are you here?" Aaminah looked away. "Long story," she mumbled under her breath.

I leaned over. "Be fair; I told you my story."

Aaminah closed her eyes. "I don't belong here, Klaus, I really don't." I nodded my head and responded. "Neither do I, Aaminah. Please tell me how you got in here." Aaminah took a deep breath. "So, my story really aggravates me because when I tell it, it just disgusts me how people can be so prejudiced, especially towards a person they know nothing about."

Aaminah paused and gritted her teeth. Then she continued. "So, one day I was at school. I go to school wearing a hijab, I mean, I am a Muslim woman. In fact, I was the only Muslim girl at my school. I was sitting in class, and there was always a group of white boys behind me yelling racist slurs and always provoking me. They always picked on me. They even tried to rip off my hijab a few times. You see, my mother had taught me how to fight, and on top of that, I took self-defense classes, so I *could* have defended myself."

Blood began to fall from Aaminah's nose. I noticed it and tried to wipe her nose with my sleeve. But she quickly stopped me. "I'm fine," Aaminah responded with a weak smile as she wiped the blood from her nose. She continued. "One day, I had had enough. I got one of my pencils and stabbed the hand of one of the boys trying to snatch off my hijab. I didn't get in trouble though, since the principal knew me and knew that I was giving those morons what they deserved, I got off with a warning. Lucky me, right? Wrong. They kept on harassing me daily.

"Spring break comes up. Two weeks later, I'm back in that *awful* class doing my work. Fifty minutes later, the bell rings, and I grabbed my backpack on my way to my next class. My backpack seemed a bit heavier than usual, but I didn't pay any attention to it. I kept on walking down the hallway, and I hear this announcement saying that they're going to be doing backpack checks and that if you're clean, there shouldn't be a problem. So, I stopped in my tracks as police filled the empty spots of our hallway and patted kids down.

"When they got to me, first they checked my hijab, then my waist, and then my shoes. I mean, I thought it was a *backpack* search but whatever. Then finally the policemen got to my backpack. I wasn't worried because I was clean. I would never be so stupid to bring anything like drugs or weapons to school. But… as they were checking my bag, I started to get a bad feeling inside.

"I remembered my backpack seemed heavier than usual. Then… then I saw it. They opened the hidden pouch at the back of my backpack and pulled out what looked like a homemade bomb. I didn't understand. It wasn't mine, and I knew exactly what type of bomb it was. This was the type of bomb that would be strapped to women, who would then be sent to populated areas in order to inflict pain and suffering. The one thing that I never thought that I would possess: a suicide bomb.

"The minute the cops pulled the bomb out everyone was told to evacuate. Two cops turned to me with a look of horror like, 'you were really gonna take out a whole school of children.' Before they put me in handcuffs, I was already planning my escape. Then these two built policemen dragged me down the hallway. As they were doing that, my hijab was slipping off. I was yelling at them to put me down, or I would sue for racial profiling. The men were holding my arms so tightly that I thought they would just snap in half.

"They lifted me, and the top part of my hijab was caught on the door screw. My neck wrapped around my hijab and I was losing breath. I was hanging from the door, and the two cops slowly backed away from me, as if I deserved it. "As I was losing conciseness, a voice told me to wake up. The second I heard that I began to gain conciseness again. I raised my hands with my last bit of strength and snapped the neck of the Policeman closest to the door using my ability. I felt hard vibrations from behind me. The cop on the other side ran to his partner's side in distress. He shook him and realized his neck was too loose for him to be alive.

"The cop looked up and saw a woman behind the glass door frantically pounding on the glass. The cop sped over to me and took me down. It turned out that my English teacher, Mrs. Crum, was pounding on the door to tell the men to save me. Mrs. Crum knew that I couldn't have wanted to bomb the school, especially with her in it because she was like a mother to me. She had an idea so I wouldn't go to jail. She called the suicide hotline and said that I tried to kill myself so that I would come here instead and avoid prison.

"Sooner or later, they would find the bomb to be inactive and do an investigation. By the time I get out, the investigation will be done, and I'll be a free woman." Aaminah looked at me and smiled as she shrugged her shoulders. I was silent. My eyes were glued to the swing set that was in front of us. I finally spoke after twenty seconds of silence. "Did you do that?" I looked over to Aaminah in astonishment. "Did you kill the police officer?" Aaminah quickly shook her head, as tears filled her eyes. "I... I... Klaus, I don't know, everything was happening so fast. I always knew I had this gift and I just used it to save myself, I'm sorry-"

I grabbed her by the waist and pulled her in for a kiss. Her soft lips melted in my mouth as her warm hands touched my face. I put my hands on her neck as I embraced her. Then I felt a sharp pain on my wrist. Suddenly, a flash of white shot into my eyes and I started to see these unexplainable images. I saw this orange-headed very tan, curvy girl, and this tall blonde Caucasian girl burst through the entrance of the building. The redhead raised her hands and began to throw items across the room just by moving her hands in different directions.

She appeared to have a symbol like mine on her wrist. As soon as I noticed the symbol, Aaminah quickly pulled out of my grip. She was hesitant to speak as I sat there in shock. She got off the bench and started pacing back and forth. I stepped off the bench table and grabbed her shoulders to keep her from pacing. "You're like me, aren't you?" She put her face in her palms. "Klaus, there's no way." She grabbed my wrist. Aaminah traced my symbol and rubbed my wrist. "What's your ability?" She asked as she rubbed her lips together.

"You liked that kiss?" I asked confidently as we stood there in the cold. Aaminah smiled and looked away. "I asked you a question first," Aaminah spoke softly as she held my hand. I smiled and looked at the door, as she still held my wrist. "Yeah, I can um, I can reverse time." She backed away from me slowly.

She turned to the bench and scraped her hand on the nail poking out from the bench. "Ughh," Aaminah grunted in pain. "What are you doing?" I asked with a concerned look on my face. She stood up and held up her hand. "Reverse time to when my hand wasn't wounded, then I'll believe you." I shook my head in confusion. "But you won't-" Aaminah cut in. "I'll remember." Aaminah finished my sentence, as she closes her eyes.

I looked at her before I turned around and backed away from her. I looked down and closed my eyes. I concentrated harder and harder, as I felt my head pound. When I opened my eyes, I was in front of Aaminah. I looked down at her hand. It was completely healed. A wave of relief rushed over me. Aaminah stood there looking at her hand in amazement. "So, you're like me," Aaminah said, playfully punching me in the arm.

"Well, I *did* tell you," I responded with my shoulders shrugged. We got back on the bench and resumed our conversation. But this time, we were sitting close together. I sat back on my palms and sighed as I took all this in, one breath at a time. "So, you're hiding here?" I asked. She nodded her head. "Practically. But the only thing is that I don't know the *genius*, rather *geniuses*, who planted the bomb in my backpack."

"Who?"

Aaminah took a deep breath and folded her hands. "Those white boys who always harassed me in class. I stabbed one of their little *cult members*, and they plant a *whole* damn bomb in my backpack to frame me. I mean, jeez, talk about *going to the extreme*."

Aaminah said as she rubbed her head in frustration. "Aaminah." She looked up at me. "Yeah, what is it?" I looked over to the door. Aaminah saw me looking and asked me what was wrong. I looked at her, as chills went up to my spine. "You know the vision; I saw while we were…"

Aaminah smiled and responded. "Yeah, I saw it too, Klaus, but what is it?" I continued looking at the door. "What if that's happening right now?" With that said, we both jumped from the bench and headed straight for the door. As Aaminah pulled open the door slightly to look through it, my birthmark started to itch out of control. Aaminah noticed and grabbed my wrist. "How long has your wrist been itching like this?" I took a while to respond. "I don't know, ever since the day I turned fifteen, I guess. So that was like, two weeks ago." Aaminah looked me in the eye. "It's happening; the rapture will come forth and this world as we know it will seize to exist." I was completely lost. "Aaminah, what are you even talking ab-" "There's no time to explain. Let's just get out there and warn the others."

We peeked through to look. It seemed like the coast was clear. We slowly opened the door and entered the facility. Nobody noticed that we were gone, except for Calvin, who had a huge grin on his face and two thumbs up as we made our way back to the table. What Aaminah just said itched at my brain. What possibly could she mean by "our world will seize to exist." My gut tells me something big is about to take place, something that I'm not ready for.

Chapter Eight-Teen

avina opened her eyes to a bright red roof. She began to look all around her. Loud sirens filled her ears as she clenched her fist. Pain filled her arms as she moved. "Where, am I?" Davina managed to ask through the pain. To her left sat two young men in uniform. Davina could barely move due to the strings attached to her chest and arms. She noticed that the men just stared at her; neither of them had answered her question.

The men sitting beside her started to notice she was moving. She watched them as they adjusted the monitor and pumped air into Davina's gas mask. Davina notices that her chest was exposed and her breathing was getting faster as the monitor started beeping.

"She's probably startled, someone calms her down," one of the men informed as a woman walked in. The woman was short and skinny, and her hair was long and dark. She could have been Prishna's twin if not for the dimple on her left cheek. She leaned into Davina's face. She picked up Davina's arm and scratched at the symbol on her wrist.

"Everything's going to be alright, don't worry. We are just gonna run a couple's test on you and figure this whole thing out." Davina looked down at her wrist. As soon as she did, she froze in shock. Her symbol was glowing a bright, piercing blue.

I lay there shaking as this woman held onto my wrist, poking at my symbol as it continued to shine.

"Unbelievable, just incredible." The woman looked into my eyes and smiled. "You are going to help scientist all over discover just what this universe is hiding from us." I shook my head in fear. The woman just giggled to herself and dropped my hand. She reached for the oxygen tank. "Get some sleep; we'll be arriving shortly."

This can't be happening. I've heard of situations like this where they find someone with supernatural abilities and do experiments on them till the day they die. I can't end up like that; I can't let them take me. I looked around to find Octavia. To my surprise, she was right behind the woman reaching for the tank. I looked around at the men watching me. I had just enough strength in me to take them down. But my only concern was how Octavia would handle it. *Would she get scared?* I shook my head. She saw me survive getting hit by a truck. I'm sure she'll be fine.

I made eye contact with Octavia, and at that moment, Octavia knew. We weren't just fighting to escape, we were fighting for our lives, and it was go time. I slowly sat up on the bed, taking off my oxygen mask. I nodded my head at Octavia as she raised the special aid kit to the woman's head. "NOW OCTAVIA!" I quickly got up and ripped the heart monitor strings from my chest and arms. I raised my hands and flung the monitor and knocked it on the heads of the three men in front of me. Octavia hit the woman in the head with the aid kit. Octavia must not have hit her hard enough because she got right back up.

The woman turned around and scrambled for a needle to inject Octavia. I ran to her defense and tackled the Woman. "OCTAVIA, CAN YOU DRIVE?" Octavia spun around and nodded her head while taking a needle. She disappeared into the darkness to go take out the driver. I grabbed the needle out of the woman's hand and injected it into her neck. She looked me in the eyes. A smile started to grow on her lips as she slowly went unconscious. I got a sickening feeling as I looked at the woman. Suddenly, the ambulance started to swerve and jump up and down.

I flipped in the air and landed on my side. "Ouch!" I screeched, as I hit the side of the bed with a loud **BANG**. *Octavia's in trouble!* I ran to the front of the ambulance to find three more men restraining her. I raised my hands and closed my eyes. I was about to try something new. Something I never knew would **work**. I raised my arms and made a grabbing motion with my fingers. My head began to pound as blood fell from my eyes. The men on top of Octavia began to scream in agony as they dropped to the floor holding on to their heads. Blood started to drip from their ears. I kept going. I could feel the horrified look from Octavia; these men were still going to be alive, they just wouldn't remember meeting us.

When all the screaming stopped, Octavia was controlling the steering wheel while I shut off all the communication systems in the ambulance.

"You know, it's not long before the hospital sends people out to look for this ambulance," I informed, as I sat in the seat next to her and drank the bottle of water that was in one of the cup holders. "I know, what are we gonna do?" Octavia asked. I went to the back of the truck to look for my shirt. "We need to blend in for now." I grabbed two firefighter hats from the back and handed one to Octavia. "Ugh great, there's blood all over my favorite sweater." I rolled my eyes as I put on my sweater and made my way back to the front where Octavia was. "Here, put your hair in a ponytail and wear this." I handed Octavia a hat. Octavia did look older than she was, maybe we could pass as firefighters. Octavia shook her head. "Why is there firefighter gear in an ambulance?" I shrugged my shoulders. I looked at Octavia and pondered. "Why did demons come after your parents if you don't have a special ability?"

As I asked, Octavia's face turned red. "In all honesty, my parents were awful, they tortured me, and even in death they still managed to ruin my life." Octavia continued. "So, in my case, demons probably came after my parents because they were stupid enough to play with an Ouija board." I shook my head and rubbed Octavia's back. "It's okay, girl, we have each other now." I felt the need to cry. I was still in shock that my whole foster family was potentially taken by demons. But I had to be strong, for Octavia and for myself.

I reached down into one of the cup holders. I pulled out a red lipstick. I looked in the mirror and put some on. I put up my hair in a high ponytail, taming my curls. I began to put some on Octavia. I guess she got startled because she swerved a little. "Davina, what the hell!" Octavia yelled. "Keep looking at the road while I put this on you." Octavia quickly shook her head. "This is so unsanitary. You don't know where that woman's lips have been." A smile grew on my face.

"What are you smiling at?" Octavia threw a fit. I giggled as I replied. "Oh, I have *plenty* of ideas where that woman's lips have been." I started to laugh as Octavia looked at the road in disgust. "Chill, Octavia I didn't mean it like that, jeez woman. Now keep still so I can make us look grown." I shook my head and let out a deep breath as I concentrated on Octavia's lips. "Voila, you look très très belle ma chere." Octavia looked at me in confusion. "What?" Octavia laughed as she put her eyes back on the road. "I just called you hot in French." *You're welcome.* I put on my firefighter hat and studied the GPS in front of me. "Alright let me see something."

I found where we were and looked at all the buildings in our path. Something caught my eye. *Backer Act Center…* I read as I adjusted my hat. "That's it!" I exclaimed and put the GPS in front of Octavia. "Let's go to this Backer Act Center, plead suicidal, and take refuge there before we decide our next move." Octavia shook her head in disapproval. "I doubt it's that easy, Davina. I mean, what are we gonna do with this ambulance?"

I looked out the window in search of a safe spot. As I did, we came to a red light. "Wait, you're not supposed to stop, don't ambulances pass through red lights?" I asked as Octavia's eyes were glued to the road. "Honestly, I have no clue, Davina." I turned to my right and saw an elderly man looking right at us. I swatted Octavia's shoulder so she could act the part.

We both looked at the elderly man and smiled as we tilted are hats in unison. He saluted us, so I guess we did something right. I never noticed how loud the sirens were until we were stuck in traffic. "Why do I feel like we stick out more than me at any birthday party?" I looked at Octavia in wonder. "Why would that be?" I asked. "I'm, I'm really tall, Davina." "Ooh, oh right, right." We sat there as the sirens hollered through the street. Sweat began to fall from Octavia's head. I could feel her fear. I turned to the rearview mirror to check if we were being followed. "We *need* to get out of here," I said under my breath.

Octavia started to shake. "Why? What do you see?" I slapped the horn and stepped on the brakes. "DAVINA, ARE YOU IN-SANE?" The ambulance went full speed as I sat on top of Octavia and took control of the steering wheel. "They're behind us; they're behind us, **THEY'RE BEHIND US!**" She pushed me off her and stepped on the gas. "I got this." She took a sharp turn and head-ed straight toward the Backer Act Facility. "They're catching up to us, Octavia!"

Octavia nodded her head. "I know! I know!" Octavia pointed to an empty lot and began to speed up. "Wait, are you sure we can stop there?" I asked as I quickly took off my hat. "I'm pretty sure."

"Look! There's a gate so we can lock them out." Octavia swirled into the parking lot and put the ambulance in the park. We jumped out and let our hair loose. I wiped my lipstick off and took a shirt off the back of the ambulance. Octavia jumped out and noticed what I was doing. Her eyes wid-ened. "No, don't wear an ambulance shirt!"

"What the heck? That's so obvious." Oc-tavia took off her sweater and gave it to me. "Here, wear this, and hurry up, Davina, we don't have much time." I nodded my head as I put on her sweater. We began to run into the bushes. Octavia pulled on my hand. "Wait! What about the people in the ambulance?" I responded slowly as I grabbed Octavia's face. "Octavia, listen to me, what you did back there was self-defense, okay? I know this all looks crazy right now, but trust me, the people that attacked us are still alive, I didn't kill them." Octavia nodded her head and grabbed my hand. "I trust you. We're in this together alright." I smiled as my dimples sunk into my cheeks.

Octavia turned around. People we're near the ambulance. "Okay, we need to go **now**!" I whispered as I dragged Octavia through the bushes. We ran and ran until we were certain we weren't being followed. We stopped to catch our breath as we arrived at the entrance. "Okay, we need a plan." I pushed the words out of my dry throat. Octavia looked at me, then turned back around and bent down to catch her breath. "We just can't walk in there and say we're suicidal." Octavia raised her hand to motion that I should stop talking while she caught her breath.

"Come on, Octavia, we don't have the time." Octavia began to sway back and forth. I ran to her side to catch her. "Please, Octavia, breathe." I pushed on Octavia's chest. Soon enough, Octavia got up and took in a long breath of air. "I'm good I'm good," Octavia assured me. I let out a long breath of relief and walked up to the entrance, still pulling Octavia along with me. "Okay, I have a plan," Octavia said as she rang the bell on the door.

"What is it?" I whispered. "Just watch."

As we stood there, a kind looking Caucasian woman, opened the door. She gave us the strangest look. I understood why; Octavia and I looked like **complete** opposites. Octavia looked at me, then back at the woman. She pulled up her sleeves to expose cut marks that led all the way up to her shoulders. I couldn't believe my eyes. Octavia looked to the ground as she covered her arm. I looked up at the woman and pulled Octavia close. "Ma'am, we need assistance."

Chapter
Nineteen

Mazikeen sat up on her bed, rolling the dice that the nurse gave her. She Tossed the dice up in the air and caught it just before they could fall to the floor. Mazikeen sat there as boredom filled her body. She attempted to get up from the bed, but the pain kept her. She laid her head on her warm, soft pillow, as she attempted to drift off into a deep sleep.

Suddenly, voices filled Mazikeen's head. She tried to make out the voices as they got louder and louder. Two minutes went by with Mazikeen's head in her pillow while she rocked back and forth. She held her breath and attempted to make out what the voices were saying. She held onto her wrist and focused on every word that was being said. *"Are you sure she's one of them? You do not want to take the wrong soul!"* Mazikeen pulled her head out of her pillow and took a breath of air. Mazikeen's instincts started to tingle. Whatever was being said was about her. Her eyes made their way to the exit sign. Mazikeen's body grew cold as she held the dice tightly in her hand.

*I **need** to get out of here,* I thought, as I held the dice tightly. *How am I gonna muffle my scream?* I took the pillowcase off the pillow and stuffed it in my mouth. I wiped the sweat from my forehead and jammed the remainder of the pillowcase deep into my mouth. I scooted my legs off the bed to prepare for my landing. I sucked up the pain and jumped off the bed and landed on my side. "OUCH!" I hollered as loud as I could as tears rushed down my face. But since I was muffled I doubt anyone could hear me. I sat on the floor and punched my leg. The pain was unbearable, but if I could walk, I could make it. I heard a small crack. My father always told me that if I ever popped a bone out of its socket, endure the pain and pop it right back in.

So, I closed my eyes and popped my leg back in. I bit down on the pillowcase so hard

I think I might have bit through it. I then managed to get up. Limping, I made my way to the door.

As my hand reached the doorknob, a powerful force pushed me back. A Nurse walked in with a pentagram on her chest. She had an odd-looking knife in her hand as she approached me. I wasn't going to let her do this. I looked up at her and analyzed the situation. *So, this woman wants to take my soul because I have superhuman abilities? How does this even work?* I need to put up a fight if I'm going to survive on earth, and I'm not about to be taken out by a possessed nurse. I pushed the bed in her path as I grabbed a book and swatted the book in her way.

She drew her knife down into the book. I saw that the knife was stuck in the book. I saw this as an opportunity. I threw the book over the bed and tackled her. I punched her repeatedly till she didn't move. Then I got off her, and I felt for her pulse. *Thank God, she's still breathing.* I quickly got up and limped over to the door. *Just my luck,* I thought as I backed up from the door. It was locked. I sat on the floor with my back against the wall, thinking of how to escape.

Aaminah and I sat at the table. Calvin scooted near me and shook me vigorously. "Dude, you were gone for a full 30 minutes!" I smiled as I rubbed my forehead. "Were we really?" Aaminah asked in surprise. Calvin looked over at both of us. "You're kidding me, right? How did you two not get caught?"

Aaminah and I just shrugged our shoulders. I had to say something to Calvin. I turned to Calvin and leaned in. "Look, I have something really important to tell you, and you can't freak out either." Calvin's eyes grew. "No, no way, Klaus, you didn't." My face fell flat as I sat back in my seat.

Aaminah pulled Calvin's shirt collar across the table till their noses practically touched. "Hey, girly, one guy at a time." Aaminah rolled her eyes. "This is serious, Calvin. You and everyone in here could be in great danger." Calvin looked at me and pointed at Aaminah. "Do you see this girl? I think she smokes more than **I** do, yeesh." Aaminah pushed Calvin back down. His back hit the chair with a hard *thud.* "Ahhh, you're stronger than you look. Wait, no, yeah you look as strong as you are, never mind." Aaminah gave him the death stare. I quickly changed the subject. "Anyway, what's our next move, Aaminah?" Aaminah's eyes watered as she frantically tried to get out of her seat.

Calvin looked at what Aaminah was looking at. He got up from the table and slowly backed away.

At first, I was confused what they were all freaking out about. I looked down at my wrist. As soon as I did, I started to experience a pounding headache. I couldn't believe my eyes. The birthmark on my wrist was shining a bright, vibrant light blue. "Klaus, what kind of infection do you have?" Calvin went on. "If I were you, I would sue that tattoo artist man, because this is just trippy." Aaminah shook her head. "That isn't a tattoo, Cline.

It's a special symbol." Aaminah ran to me. "What did you see?" She held my head as she closed her eyes. She began to shake as she chanted these odd words, *familiar* sounding words. If I wasn't mistaken, these words sound like the words I heard when I walked passed the girl's bathroom. *Is it possible that Aaminah could have already seen this moment?* I thought to myself, as her hands pressed on my head. I heard a loud gasp, as Aaminah pulled away from me. "There are others, others like us." I looked over at Calvin. His face looked so shocked I couldn't help but laugh. Aaminah slammed her hand on the table to get our silence. The minute she did, both Cline and I jumped up in are seats. Aaminah sat back down and folded her hands together. She pointed to the entrance across from us. "Klaus, watch that door."

I nodded my head and faced the door. All three of us watched the door closely, as two girls stepped into the building. Calvin slowly turned to Aaminah. "How did you… never mind, at this point, I've seen it all," Calvin said, with no emotion as he sat back in his chair. I looked over at Aaminah and shook my head. "Aaminah, that's not them. They don't have the symbol." I pointed to the tall blonde girl behind the desk.

Aaminah redirected my finger to the *mixed raced* girl with orange hair. "Her. That's the one." Aaminah, let go of my arm. I was still so lost because the girl she was pointing to had no symbol either. I brought that to Aaminah's attention. A look of shock spread across her face. "Hold on; you mean to tell me you don't see that girl's symbol in plain sight on her wrist?" I nodded my head. "We need to get them over here." Both Aaminah and I looked back at Calvin.

"What? I mean, to know for sure if that's even really them, you need to meet them, right?" I slowly nodded my head. I was impressed once again; I'm pretty sure that was the smartest thing I'd ever heard Calvin say since I met him. "I'll go over to them and bring them to our table," Aaminah informed, as she got up.

Calvin and I watched Aaminah walk up to the two girls. They were hesitant, but sure enough, they followed her back to our table. The two girls slowly sat down in front of us. An awkward silence filled the table, but the ginger with freckles broke it. "Hi, my name's Davina, and this is Octavia." Everyone at the table said their "Hi's," except for me; I couldn't. As I attempted to talk, my wrist felt as if it was being squeezed.

Davina looked over at me in wonder. "Hey… are you alright?" I slowly nodded my head. But I wasn't okay; I felt like my whole body was burning from the inside. I put my head down. Octavia looked my way. She gasped and jumped out of her chair and fell back. "Oh my gosh, Davina, look!" Davina then turned her head to see what Octavia was yelling about. "There's nothing there Octavia, chill." Octavia got back up and sat at the table. Calvin turned to Octavia and smiled.

Octavia looked up at Calvin and let out a short giggle. "Ha, in your dreams," Octavia mumbled under her breath. I noticed that Davina didn't look so good either. Aaminah cut the greeting short. "Alright, I never liked small talk so let's cut the chit-chat and get straight to the point." Calvin turned to Aaminah and shook his head. "How rude." Octavia noticed Davina's distress. "Davina, what's wrong?" Davina itched her wrist, and then Calvin grabbed Davina's wrist. "Klaus, you mean to tell me you can't see that this girl's wrist is glowing. It's doing the same thing your wrist is doing." Despite my pain, I glanced over at her wrist. "I can't see any-thing." Aaminah grabbed both my wrist and Davina's wrist. Aaminah closely observed Davina's symbol. "It's different. Your sym-bol isn't the same."

Aaminah placed her hand on the table and closed her eyes. "Wait, this all makes sense." She opened her eyes. "You're part of a group. Different symbols for different abilities, but your bare eyes can't see each other's symbols." She turned to her right and looked at a room with windows all around it. "My magnifying glass, it's in there, one of you has to go get it so I can prove to you that you two are both targets."

I got up and moved away from the table. Suddenly, my pain stopped completely. I looked at Davina. Her pain had stopped too. "Let's keep our distance for now," I told Davina, as I walked to the other end of the table. "Wait, there should be no reason why you guys would feel any pain." Aaminah held Davina's hand. "Are there others like you?"

Davina shook her head no. "Honestly I don't know at this point." "Do you have an ability," Aaminah asked, as she set down Davina's hand.

"I do, but if I show you, it'll attract too much attention to us." Davina looked at Octavia while Aaminah looked at me for answers. "Give me a minute." I began to think.

Suddenly, it hit me. *Wait a minute, that girl in my dreams!* I slammed my hand on the table to get Aaminah's attention. "Aaminah, there was a girl you were telling me about earlier. She was outside covered in blood." Aaminah's eyes grew big as she nodded her head. "I had dreams about her falling from space. I think she might be in this facility."

Aaminah sat there holding Davina's wrist. "We can only know with the magnifying glass." Davina gave me a lost look. "Space? Are you serious?" I nodded my head. Aaminah pointed at the room she was talking about before. "Go in there and act like you need to speak with the counselor. Then when she's not looking, go in her drawer and look for a vintage magnifying glass with a brown wooden handle." "I got this," Davina responded as if she was at war. Now that I think about it, she was. We **all** were.

Chapter Twenty

I tapped on the glass, as I studied the pictures on the wall. I peeked through the glass in search of the desk Aaminah was talking about. Before I could step back from the door, the woman sitting inside the office told me to enter. I opened the door and calmly entered the room. The woman was sitting there with her hands folded, waiting for me to sit on one of the office chairs. I made my way over to one of the chairs. "Do you need help sleeping? Is that why you came here?"

I sat down and wiggled to get comfy in the chair before answering. "Actually, I came to discuss some issues I've been having about cutting." I could tell I got the woman's attention. She stopped what she was doing on her computer, faced me, and took off her glasses. "What seems to be the problem?" She asked as she reached into her desk. My eyes followed her hands as they passed over the magnifying glass. She pulled out a notepad and a pen before shutting the desk drawer. She clicked the pen and assumed the position.

I hesitated to speak, as I needed to think up a story to tell. Then it hit me. "I was informed that you had some books that could help me stop cutting," I said as sorrowfully as I could. The woman wrote down what I said. "Why do you cut yourself, Davina?" I was taken aback when the woman said my name. I looked around the room for something to use, anything. But then I thought of Octavia and seeing those cuts on her arms. Even though I had only known her for a brief time, I still felt the pain. So, I used that feeling. I used that pain.

"Sometimes I feel like I'm worth nothing, like the feeling of not being wanted consumes me." The woman wrote every word I said down. My eyes kept a locked stare at the desk. I continued. "I feel numb inside, so I pierce my skin, hoping that I'll feel any pain, and then when I do… when I feel the pain, in a way, it's like a feeling of release." My eyes began to water. I batted my eyelashes to stop tears from forming in my eyes. The woman wrapped up the paragraph she was writing and shut her notepad. She carefully placed it on the desk and folded her hands.

"Davina, I'm so sorry to hear that you are going through all of this." I gave her an awkward smile as I slowly nodded my head in guilt. She leaned in closer to me and continued. "Luckily for you, I do have a book that should help you at least think before your self-harm." The woman got up from the desk and pushed in her chair. "Sit here patiently dear; I'll be right back."

I watched the woman as she left the room and went into an adjacent room. I noticed some motion out of the corner of my eye. I glanced over to the table through the window of the room. Klaus and everyone else at the table was giving me the thumbs-up sign.

I could see Calvin and Octavia frantically directing me to the desk. They looked nuts while doing it. I nodded frantically back in understanding, as I got up and headed toward the table drawer. I looked back to see if the woman was heading back. When I didn't see her, I turned back around and resumed opening the drawer.

My hands felt a familiar feeling as I grabbed the magnifying glass. I held the magnifying glass firmly in my hands. I attempted to look through it, but the moment I tried, my wrist began to burn. I looked over to Aaminah in shock. She motioned for me to come back.

I looked at the door and noticed a shadow approaching the door. I ran back to my seat and stuffed the magnifying glass in my bra. As my butt hit the seat, the woman from earlier walked right back in. I observed her holding two heavy looking textbooks in her arms. She managed to sit back down with the load. *I must get out there*, I thought, as I conjured up an excuse to leave. I sat up in my chair and took a deep breath. "Ma'am, I don't feel comfortable talking about this anymore." I slowly got up and headed for the door. "That's understandable, sweetheart, just come back when you're ready." I softly smiled at the woman before shutting the door behind me.

I made eye contact with Klaus as I made my way back to the table. He had the most beautiful eyes. I stared at him the whole walk back to the table. I shook my head to stop myself. *Davina snap out of it*! I thought to myself as I sat down across from him. "Pull it out, let me see it." Aaminah pounced on me with excitement. As everyone anxiously awaited the presentation of the magnifying glass, I sat there still. "Alright, boys turn around, or don't and get slapped," I informed, as I stuck my hands in my bra.

"Oh, then I guess I'll keep watching and take my chances," Calvin said, as he gave me a side smile. Octavia slapped the back of his head and shoved him to turn around. I kept on feeling in my bra, but I couldn't find it. *Great. Just great,* I thought, as I ran my hands through my full head of hair. *What was I thinking putting something in my bra? I'm flat-chested, so really, I should've seen this coming.* I looked over to Aaminah. Calvin and Klaus turned around. "What the-" Calvin wondered, as he looked at Aaminah. Her eyes were rolled back as she chanted in a different language. "What do you see?" Klaus shook Aaminah. As soon as he did, Aaminah's eyes rolled back in place, and she gasped for air as she tightly held her chest.

"Someone picked up the Magnifying glass; evil is surrounding it." I rolled my eyes and got up out of my seat.

I got up and leaned in so everybody at the table could hear me. "The suspense is killing me," I said. "I wanna know why my wrist glows on and off and where my foster family disappeared to, so we NEED to find this thing and fast." I patted the table as I sat back down. Klaus nodded his head. "Alright, Aaminah, what do we have to do?" Aaminah got up and pointed to the staff behind us. "They have it, if we can get the magnifying glass from them, without them seeing us, then we're safe." I raised an eyebrow. "Safe, what's that supposed to mean?" I looked around, as no one spoke another word. "We're not safe." Aaminah slowly shook her head. "Not to get all religious on you, but have you heard of the Rapture?" Everyone nodded their heads.

"Wow, okay. Well, the rapture took place yesterday. To my understanding, we are doomed unless we change decisions made in the past." Calvin cut in. "So, what now, we're gonna go back in time and stop Eve from giving Adam the forbidden grapefruit?" Octavia snickered at Calvin's slick commentary. I rolled my eyes. I looked over at Aaminah, as Octavia sat there wide-eyed and amused. "Davina, we are a team." Klaus shook his head. "Not without the other girl we're not."

Octavia spoke up. "Let's go get that glass."

We all got up and made our way to the front of the Backer Act Center. I looked over the desk. I hit Klaus in the arm. "*Ouch,* what is it?" I quickly pointed to the magnifying glass. "Look. It's in someone's purse." I looked up and noticed a man was walking our way. "What do all of you youngins need?" "*Youngins,*" Calvin mocked the man under his breath. The man looked over at Calvin. I quickly cut in before he could do any damage.

"Sir, we were just wondering if our parents sent us any clothes yet." The man turned around. Calvin began to reach for the magnifying glass. "*No smart one, not yet!*" Octavia whispered as she pushed him back. They walked back to the cubbies where facility clothes were placed. He checked the cubes and saw nothing. He then entered another room. "NOW." I mouthed to Klaus, as he quickly snatched the magnifying glass out of the purse.

Aaminah and Octavia kept watch, as Klaus put the glass in his pocket. I turned my head to see a brown door. Something was telling me to go toward it. But I had to fight that feeling. If anyone saw me, it could mess everything up. I looked away from the door and backed away from the front desk.

"Where are you going?" Calvin grabbed my arm and pulled me back up to the front. "I need to ask Aaminah something!" Calvin shook his head. "Nah, you're supposed to be acting like you're asking this guy where your clothes are. I'll ask her for you." The man walked up to us. "I'm sorry, but I couldn't find any clothes that were left for any of you." I nodded my head and gave the man a big cheesy smile. "No, it's fine, thanks for checking." I looked over to Calvin. His face was pale as if he had seen a ghost. He was holding up the magnifying glass to his eye. "Oh, *hell* Nah," he said, as Calvin shook his head lowering the magnifying glass. "Is this man supposed to be glowing like that?"

Calvin asked as Aaminah looked through the glass.

"Don't look at them." Aaminah's eyes grew big. "They're here." Aaminah looked around and shook. She then lowered the magnifying glass in terror. "We need to get out of here, and fast." Calvin waved his hands blocking Aaminah. "Wait, why can't we look at the demons?" Aaminah shot him a dull look. "Hear yourself, if you look at them and they feel you are looking, they'll take your soul." Aaminah smiled a comical smile and looked away from Calvin. I took the magnifying glass out of Aaminah's hand and pointed it towards Klaus's wrist.

As I pointed it, my wrist began to sting. "Ouch, ouch, ouch!" I exclaimed, as I backed away and rubbed my wrist on my leg. I looked up at Klaus in amazement. He smiled back at me. "You saw it!" I nodded my head as I handed him the glass. He held it to my wrist. "Does your symbol hurt?" He slowly shook his head as he studied my wrist. "Wait, your symbol looks just like Aaminah's. That's weird."

My eyes again led me to the brown door. I looked down at Klaus examining my symbol. He looked back up at me. "Now that I think out it, you and Aaminah do look similar. Do you guys have the same ability?" I shrugged my shoulders. "Aaminah can see into the future. *I* can only see into the past and control certain things with my mind." Aaminah snatched the magnifying glass and began to point to people all around the room. "She's a demon, so is he, and so is she." Aaminah shook her head and looked at all of us. "It's time to fight for your lives, are you ready?"

Calvin burst out in laughter. "For all that, I'm ready for anything," Calvin responded, pointing to Octavia. Octavia looked up and scoffed. Aaminah looked at Klaus and me. I looked back at her. I noticed the symbol on her neck. I was confused. *How come I can see her symbol, but I can't see Klaus's.* I looked over to Aaminah once more and took a deep breath. *I need to know.* I walked up to Aaminah and quickly put my wrist on her neck. "No don't!" Klaus shouted. Both my eyes and Aaminah's eyes rolled back, as we saw our connection.

September 17th, Eleven years back

Aaminah and Davina's parents stood in the kitchen discussing their concerns as Davina and Octavia lay asleep on the rug, surrounded by blankets, toys, and books. Evoca and Francis, *Davina's parents*, made their way to the table. Francis sat down as Evoca stood up to chopped onions for dinner. "When are you going to get help, Reviv?" Francis asked Octavia's mother.

Reviv looked over at Octavia sleeping next to Davina. "I don't need help; I'm not marked like you, okay? "I didn't move to Ireland to die at the hands of evil." Aaminah's mother hissed. Francis nodded his head in understanding. "I know Reviv, but you are my wife's sister, Evoca worries about you." Reviv rolled her eyes. "He's right, you know. I do care about you." Evoca replied. Niahm, Aaminah's father cut in. "We can give Aamiah away. I can't stand to see her being followed by the evil that lurks within us."

Evoca shook her head as tears fell from her eyes. "I couldn't; I couldn't give Davina away. I'd rather have her kill me than end up killing herself." Evoca continued. "In two years, the evil will take over us. There's nothing we can do about that, but what we can do is change the fate for our children." Francis held on to Evoca's shoulders as she continued. "I'm keeping my child, Reviv. Francis and I fight sometimes, but we'll make it through the next two years and keep Davina safe as long as we can."

Niamh stood up and hugged Francis. "You're my brother, so I'll do what I can to protect my niece." Francis smiled and ruffed Niamh's hair. Reviv turned to Evoca. "Now whose plan was it to marry Irish brothers again?" They both laughed as they hugged each other. Reviv held her sister's hand. "I respect your decision to keep Davina. Just be careful, don't forget to give her the knife when the time comes." Evoca nodded her head and looked over to Davina. Reviv joined her. "It's so not fair. How come your baby comes out with bright orange hair and mine doesn't?" Revive jokingly asked as she held Evoca close.

"Because I married the redhead and you married the strong head?" Evoca stated, as her sister laughed beside her. "Do you think it was stupid to marry at 19, leave Haiti, and get our selves into all this mess?" Evoca wondered out loud while Reviv kissed both Aaminah and Davina on the forehead. "Maybe, but we would have never known until we tried, right?" Evoca smirked and turned to her husband. Revive noticed and playfully shoved Evoca's arm. "And we sure did, huh?" Evoca smiled and answered back. "Yeah, we sure did."

As the vision ended, both Aamianh and I gasped for air. Klaus ran to our side. "What the heck did you guys do?" I looked over at Aaminah and tackled her. "OUR MOTHERS WERE SISTERS!"

Aaminah smiled and hugged me. "I actually have a family!" I squealed as tears filled my eyes. But my excitement stopped as my eyes met the brown door. I grabbed Aaminah's arm and pointed to the brown door. "What's behind that door?" Aaminah gave me a confused look. "You just find out we're cousins, and you wanna get back to work so quickly?" I turned Aaminah's head in my direction. "We need to focus." I took a deep breath and continued. "Aaminah, listen, I've been getting these vibes about that door."

Aaminah looked over to me and put her hand on my chest. "Go with your instincts, what do you see?" I looked over at Klaus. He nodded his head and motioned that I should close my eyes. I closed my eyes as my mind drifted into a state of being.

Chapter Twenty-One

"Holy cow! There's a dead woman on the floor!" Calvin hollered, as Klaus and Davina picked Mazikeen up. "She's not dead, just unconscious." Mazikeen replied. "Don't worry; we aren't demons," Davina informed Mazikeen. "I know. I wouldn't be able to do this." Mazikeen put her fingertips to the sides of her head and closed her eyes. She looked at Davina. *Is she Asian?* Then she looked over at Klaus. *I wonder what's her story.* Mazikeen took her hands from her temples then smiled. "I can read minds."

Both Klaus and Davina's eyes met as Octavia called for them outside. "There are demons coming this way so you people better hurry." Octavia hollered, as she held the magnifying glass and stood to watch at the door. "Can you guys hurry it up, the staff are attacking us, and I only took two years of judo," Octavia added on. Klaus looked back at Mazikeen. "We need to go." All together, they rushed out of the room.

I couldn't run any longer; my leg was killing me. I looked at the others fighting the staff. There was a red-headed girl with a huge head of hair moving things with her mind and throwing them everywhere, along with two others jumping in the air like it was nothing. Where did I fit in? "Hey, are you alright?" A boy with gray eyes came to my side. "Klaus, the names Klaus." I nodded. "Klaus, I like it." I looked up. There were kids running and screaming. Other kids seemed perfectly happy, while others were asleep. "Your shoelace is untied," Klaus told me.

She's so beautiful, Klaus's mind thought. I looked down at him as he was fixing my shoelaces.

"You shouldn't be thinking of such things," I replied to his thought. "I'm sorry?" Klaus replied. I looked over at a girl glaring our way. "By the look, that girl is giving me; it seems like you are already spoken for." Klaus looked at *the girl*. "She's just jealous, forgive her." I laughed and shook my head. I guess the girl heard us having too much fun because she came over. "This girl has a name you know." She wiped the blood off her hands using her shirt and tossed Klaus her weapon. "The names Aaminah. I'm one of you. Well, not *one of you*, but we're sort of linked. There's nothing but love being spread, Mazikeen, don't worry." Aaminah looked over at Klaus. "No one here is jealous."

Klaus quickly got up as another person approached him. He began to comfort a boy and told him to tell his friends to go to their rooms. Earth teenagers are so quick on their feet; they're not too different from the teen's up in the space station. "What now?" A Caucasian boy asked Aaminah. Aaminah looked around. Everyone was on the floor or panicking in the facility rooms. Staff members who weren't demons were running to their cars or screaming into small devices. The red-headed girl clapped her hands to get our attention. "Raise your hand if you know how to drive." Two Caucasian's raised their hands along with Aaminah. "Who knows how to drive *well*?" The red head looked at the blonde. The blonde Caucasian put her hand down along with Aaminah. "You're kidding me; there's no way I'm putting my life in your hands." The ginger hissed, as she jumped off the chair.

"Aye, jit, don't judge a book by its cover, I ain't crazy. I'm not like the rest of these people." Klaus shook his head. "Just because you're in a Backer Act Facility doesn't make you crazy, Cline." ***I'm not a murderer; I'm not a murderer, I'm not a murderer.*** I slowly turned my head to the Caucasian boy. He was looking to the ground wide-eyed with a clenched fist. The girl who was previously talking walked up to me and reached out her hand. "Davina, and you are?" I lost focus of the boy and smiled as I shook her hand. "Mazikeen, nice to meet you." Davina's eyes turned wide. "Oh my gosh, your accent!" I raised my eyebrows. "I have an accent?" A tall Caucasian girl shoved Davina out of the way and grabbed my hand. "If you're really from space, then why is your fashion A1?"

I wrinkled my forehead in confusion. What fashion was she talking about? I literally have on baggy, wrinkled clothing from who knows where.

"A1 as in the A1 sauce?" Klaus asked slowly. A Caucasian boy, I'm guessing by the name of Cline, ran up to me and he tugged my arm. "We need to go! I just know the cops are about to pull up. Secondly, my name is Calvin, but you can call me Cline." Calvin winked at me. Octavia cut in. "All-right, alright let's go."

I closed my eyes and focused. I saw sirens and a police vehicle on its way. "He's right, I can feel it too," I said, as I pressed on my leg. "We need to go now, guys," Octavia yelled as she opened the door. We all ran out of the Backer Act Facility. Klaus paused. "I forgot my clothes," Klaus hollered, as he ran back to his room. I stood there waiting for him. The others were in the parking lot trying to *hotwire a car*. Almost a second later, Klaus came running back with a huge bag of clothes. "Go, go, go!" Klaus motioned to the parking lot, as we ran out of the building. I could tell something wasn't right. I could tell we were about to experience something big. I just hoped we would all live through it. "It's starting up," Octavia said, as she got up from under the car. Calvin was right beside her, shocked as ever. "Now how do *you* know how to hotwire a car?"

Octavia rolled her eyes and smirked. "Don't judge a book by its cover. Isn't that right, Klaus?"

Klaus looked over at Calvin. "Right." Klaus smiled over at Octavia, as he slammed the car's trunk closed. "Very funny, using my own words against me, very mature," Calvin said, as he attempted to open the car door. *Click.* "Wow, you did good, Barbie," Aaminah commented right before she entered the car. "Why a Cadillac though?" Calvin complained as he shoved himself into the car.

"And it's a clean, bright, white, fancy car. Way to go for something not too obvious," Klaus added.

Octavia honked the horn and shouted. **"Can you ungrateful children just get in the car?"** I stood to watch near the car and looked out for any cop cars. I felt a sharp pain on my wrist. I turned around to see Klaus behind me. He pushed on my shoulder. "The car is running, let's go." I nodded my head and followed behind him. I ran to the front seat to see that it was already oc-cupied. I grunted and entered the back seat. Surprisingly, I wasn't squished. This was a HUGE Cadillac.

Aaminah was in the front seat attempting to direct Calvin to a safe house she knew. I sat alongside Mazikeen and Klaus. Octavia was in the trunk surrounded by the clothes Klaus brought. The trunk was huge, so I wasn't worried. *I bet Octavia only sat behind to avoid any questions from me about the cuts on her arms,* I thought, as I turned around to look at Octavia. But hiding from me won't be enough to get me off her back.

"So, what about that safe house, huh? What's the deal with that?" Calvin asked as he gripped the steering wheel. "This house was blessed by my mother and Davina's mother as well. It was built to keep us safe from all of this." I smiled, as Aaminah con-tinued. "My mother always used to tell me bedtime stories about this house. She even made a song with vivid and very detailed directions and sung it to me every night." "If we can get there safely, then hopefully we can survive the rapture." "A.K.A., demon apocalypse," Calvin added. I turned to Mazikeen. "So, you're from space, right?" Mazikeen nodded her head. "It's absolutely beautiful up there." Octavia spun around. "Is it just like the movies?"

Mazikeen raised an eyebrow. "Not necessarily." Mazikeen continued. "I was quite surprised to see so many new things down here on earth. I thought earth would be completely ruined. If people survived, I would expect all of you guys to be wearing brighter colors." Klaus shook his head in confusion. "Wait, wait, wait. What time do you think we are in right now?" Mazikeen hesitated. "Isn't' it 1976?"

Everyone in the car shot her a confused look. "What did they teach you up there?" Klaus jokingly asked. I cut in. "How are we living in two different worlds?" I continued. "The technology was advanced in your space station, right?" Mazikeen nodded her head. "Then why did you think we are in the 70's?" Calvin yelled out loud. "2K17 BABY!" Aaminah slapped the back of Calvin's head. "Shut your lame behind up and focus on the road," Aaminah Demanded. "Hit me again and see what happens," Calvin warned.

"Bruh, try me. Is that a threat or a promise though?" Aaminah comically responded to Calvin's threat.

I sat back in my seat watching this whole thing unfold before my eyes. I felt a sharp pain and quickly moved my hand away from Klaus's side. "Ouch, what the hell Klaus." I hollered, as I felt an excruciating pain in my wrist. "Hey, keep it down back there. Damn!" Calvin honked. "Davina, I can't help it," Klaus responded laughing. What is wrong with him? I'm in pain, and he's laughing? "Are you high? How is this funny to you, aren't you in pain?" Klaus nodded his head. "Yeah, but your reaction was funny as hell."

Aaminah jumped in. "Oh, so hell is funny to you because all sorts of demons are after us." Everyone in the car grew silent. But of course, Calvin broke the silence. "Why, these things after ya'll the hell." Klaus shrugged. "I've been having unexplainable paranormal experiences a lot lately. I'm convinced that I was possessed and the demon that possessed me tried to kill me." Klaus continued. "I woke up with no memory of what had happened one time, and then...

there was this one time on the Backer Act Facility van that a demon attacked my bus driver."

I was out of words. If what they are saying is true, the things that took our parents could be after us. "Klaus, do you have both of your parents?" Klaus nodded his head. "Why wouldn't I?"

My eyes began to get watery. Calvin cut in. "How many demons are after you guys?" Klaus and I shrugged our shoulders, but Aaminah had an answer. "Three, one for each ability." "For some reason, you three possess special in human traits that other special beings would not be able to have." So, in a case that a demon does finally find one of you, it will only take the person that has the ability they are looking for, which I hope never happens." Aaminah looks at me through the rear-view mirror. I understood what she meant. But I was still confused. "Are parents, the evil they messed with, does that have a lot to do with this?" I asked dreading. Aaminah Slowly nodded her head. "We will discuss this more in the safe house, Ok?"

Before anyone could notice, I blinked rapidly. Klaus looked over to me. His face dropped, and he noticed I wasn't okay. "Are your parents…" I nodded my head slowly. "Mine are too," Aaminah jumped in. "Same," Octavia said in a sleepy voice. "And mine…" Mazikeen added. "How did your parents die if you don't mind me asking," I asked Mazikeen. "It was absolutely traumatizing." ***HONK! HONK! "PULL OVER YOUR VEHICLE!"*** A deep voice called out from behind us.

Aaminah took a glanced at the viewfinder and hollered. "This isn't good, the cops found us!" Octavia raised her head up to see three cop cars on our trail ganging up on us. **"Step on it, Cline!"** Octavia shouted, startling all of us. "I'm trying, but as you can see, I'm driving a soccer mom car." Octavia rolled her eyes and made her way to the front of the car. "Just move." She ordered. "You for real right now, Octavia?" I asked as I put my hands on my head. "Yeah, the man is driving you can't just steal the wheel from him like that," Klaus added on. "Hey man, I got a babe on my lap, I ain't complaining."

Octavia laughed as she stomped on the gas pedal. "What the hell are you doing, blondie? You're swerving like crazy!" Octavia pushed Calvin off the seat. "Hey, watch it, Eminem, you're blonde too." Laughter filled the van. "What's an *Eminem*?" Mazikeen asked as she laughed. I couldn't stop laughing long enough to answer her question. Now that I look at him, Calvin does look a lot like Eminem. "Okay, instead of chewing on me, you people should be discussing a way to get these cops off our tail."

Aaminah pointed to the GPS. "There's a mall up ahead. If you just park in one of the empty parking spaces, then they won't know which car we are in." Everyone paused in amazement. "Damn aren't you just smart," Klaus added as he smirked at Aaminah. The car swerved, pushing us all to one side of the car. "Octavia, give the wheel back to Calvin. I never thought I'd say this, but I trust him more." I said as my face smashed against the car window. "Ugh, fine!" Octavia hissed, as she jumped off Calvin. "The chase is all yours. After all, you're not afraid," Octavia scoffed under her breath. "You just gave me my early birthday present, blondie, so I'm not even gonna chew on you." "Wait, how do we know that demons aren't chasing us?" Mazikeen asked. "Can I see the glass, Aaminah?"

Aaminah handed the magnifying glass to Mazikeen. Mazikeen turned around and looked through the glass. "One cop car is glowing a bright blue." Aaminah nodded her head. "Well, that cop car has a demon in it." Klaus beat on the car chair. "Uh, guys were going on the interstate." Aaminah quickly looked over at Calvin. Calvin gripped the steering wheel as he swerved into the other lane. He was driving faster and faster by the second. Suddenly, we saw someone on the road. I couldn't believe what I was seeing; it was Prishna.

"Oh my gosh! *Look out! It's Prishna!"* I got up from my seat and took the wheel from Calvin. "Stop, Davina, it's not her." Aaminah hollered, as we swerved to the side of the interstate above water. "Stop your vehicle now!" The man behind us in the cop car yelled, as the sirens only got louder. "We can't kill her!" Octavia yelled as she grabbed the wheel from Calvin, causing the car to steer right off the bridge.

As we hit the curb, the car flipped into the air and off the interstate. "I don't wanna die!"

Calvin screeched, as we plummeted down. "Klaus, use your ability, now!" Aaminah yelled, holding onto her seat. **"I can't."** Klaus cried out, as we tumbled in the air. I saw what was happening around me. *No, not like this,* I thought. I took Mazikeen's wrist and grabbed Klaus's hand. I nodded to him. He looked at me with fear in his eyes. He closed his eyes and held on tightly to my wrist. I felt an intense pressure against my head, and then a bright flash of light filled my eyes.

I opened my eyes to see us back on the interstate. "We did it!" I yelled as we all cheered. "Hey, why am I on Calvin's lap again?" whined Octavia. "Again, not complaining." Octavia pushed Calvin out from under her, taking full control of the wheel. "What the hell just happened?" Klaus asked as he gasped for breath. "We used all of our abilities to help strengthen yours. We made it," Davina replied, as she held Klaus's hand. I noticed this and averted my eyes from the pragmatic scene. "Look, Octavia, the mall!" Davina shouted as she put her mess of hair in a bun. "Let's pull into a parking space near the entrance," I added.

We zoomed into the parking lot and quickly parked near the entrance. There were so many cars that looked like the car we were driving. I highly doubt they'll find us… at least I hope so. "Alright, guys, pull the seats down and lay low." The minute Aaminah said that everyone did as she said, no questions asked. "If they find us, we're so dead," Octavia whispered as she shivered from the cold. "Someone turn off the car engine," Klaus instructed. Everyone was silent. "You're kidding me; no one knows how to turn off the car?" Klaus slapped his palm on his head as he wrapped himself in the clothes he had taken from the Backer Act Facility.

"We hotwired it, genius, what did you think?" Octavia scoffed while changing her shirt. "Whoa, Woah, Woah, Goldie Locks, get a room," Davina told Octavia, as she attempted to cover her. "I wish I could, but we need to change so they don't recognize us." Klaus nodded his head. "He's right; they have us on camera using our abilities." Davina put her hands on her face and took a long breath. "If they do, then they'll take us and experiment on us." I got up and looked around to see if any police cars were surrounding us. "Get down, Mazikeen; they can't see us," Davina informed. I nodded my head.

"I know, but we also need to get to the safe house as soon as possible." Aaminah looked up at me. "She's right; we can't just sit here." Klaus looked around with me. "I don't see them," Klaus said, studying the outside atmosphere. I looked around until I was certain that the cops weren't on our tail. "Alright, let's go, the coast is clear." Aaminah nodded at me with a smile and adjusted her seat. Everyone else also began to adjust their seats. "It's game time." Calvin calmly muttered under his breath. He pulled out of the mall parking lot and sped onto the road.C

Chapter Twenty-wo

"I smell like absolute crap right now," Calvin admitted, as we calmly drove on the road. "Yeah, I don't smell too fresh myself," Aaminah exclaimed while she smelled her shirt. Calvin looked over at Aaminah and smiled. "Yeah trust me, Aaminah, **I know**." Aaminah gave him a death stare right before she slapped the back of his head. Calvin just laughed and turned back to the road, not wanting any trouble.

"We really should freshen up somewhere." Octavia looked at the GPS. "Okay, so there's a gas station up ahead, let's just stop there."

Octavia looked over at Davina. She noticed that Davina wasn't her spontaneous, rude self. Octavia climbed out of the back and sat next to Davina. I scooted over; I was keeping a close ear. "Are you okay?" Octavia asked Davina, rubbing her back. "I don't know… are we Octavia? What's happening to our families? Why did I see another illusion, and why was it Prishna…?" Octavia shook her head. "They're trying to take your powers for their own use." Both Davina and Octavia turned around to see Aaminah's eyes rolled back.

"I'll never get used to that," Calvin stated, as he turned into the gas station, which wasn't all that crowded. Davina grabbed Aaminah's wrist. "What did you see?" Aaminah's eyes rolled back to normal. "You three are the three chosen ones. Three different demons seek the power you have." I looked at Davina and Davina looked at Klaus. "Why just the three of us?" I asked in curiosity. Aaminah had an answer, as usual. "We are all linked by September 20th." Aaminah continued. "But the only difference is, I'm one year older than all of you, I'm 16, and you all are 15 if I'm not mistaken."

Klaus's eye's widened. "There's no way we were all born on the same day?" Davina didn't seem surprised as she cut in. "So, this whole *demon taking over thing* is caused by us? We brought them here?" Davina asked. I only wanted to know one thing. Why did a whole space station full of people suddenly die while I survived? Aaminah continued. "We'll discuss this more at the safe house. Right now, we need to get food." "If you think about them, it'll be easier for them to navigate you."

I responded to Aaminah with the worried look I'd been holding back. She only returned my glance with an encouraging smile. "We can do this okay, all of us, we can survive this." With that said, Aaminah jumped out of the car. She tucked her knife in her left boot and walked to the gas station entrance. We all watched her as fresh air filled the car. "How did she get the pocket knife?" I asked wistfully. Octavia and Calvin shrugged. "I want a pocket knife," Calvin muttered under his breath. Klaus heard him and smiled, pushing his head to the side.

I had an uneasy feeling in my chest. I closed my eyes and concentrated on my mind. I heard voices coming from the back of the gas station. *This is what they look like. They are extremely dangerous, so keep a look out and tell your workers to do the same.* I opened my eyes and looked around for Aaminah. I quickly shook Klaus, who was beside me. "Go get Aaminah. It's not safe." Klaus shot me a frightened, concerned look and quickly stumbled out of the car. He quickly got back in and rolled down the windows. "Aaminah, get back in," Klaus called after Aaminah. Aminah looked at the window. *All will be scanned as they enter, and yes, our cameras work.*

Aaminah slowly turned around and made her way back to the car. "Screaming will only attract unwanted eyes, Klaus," Aaminah said as she reached for the bag of clothes. She ripped through it and looked through the clothes. She handed each of us a new set of clothes to wear. "Feel free to dress how you like. Just change your look, so they don't recognize us." I looked at my clothes. "Why do I have men's clothing?" I laughed, as I looked in the bag for something else. "We need a mix of looks, Mazikeen."

Davina put her hand in the bag of clothes blocking my path. "It doesn't look comfortable," I said as I laughed, fighting Davina for the bag. "You guys play too much." Klaus sighed, as he changed in the back. Suddenly,

Davina let go of the bag. "What if I dress the same to match with you?" The minute Davina said that Calvin's head whipped around faster than the speed of light. "If *anyone* is going to be the best-dressed man, it's gonna be me.

"Let me see your clothes." Octavia laughed. "No, go find your own clothes, moron." Klaus jumped in. "Or, we could just make Maze look like a K-pop star." I shot Klaus an offended look. But apparently, Davina felt the sting more because she jumped in front of me. "**Maze**, what is a *Maze*, boy? If you don't call her by her name…" I looked at Klaus in confusion. "What the hell, Klaus? Out of everybody, you had to try my-" Aaminah jumped in before I could finish my sentence. "If you people don't calm down!" The car grew silent. "I'm the one who can see flashes of the future here, so I decide who looks like what to blend in. This isn't a damn game or dress up club, and this *sure* ain't no damn costume party."

Dress up club? Calvin mouthed to himself. Klaus noticed and nudged him slightly as a side smile slid on his face. "We do what we can to survive, and if it means making

Calvin look like a drag queen, then we do it. Do I make myself clear?" The car filled with laughter as a look of shock filled Calvin's face. I nodded my head and laughed along. "You would look hot as a drag queen, Calvin." Davina winked at Calvin before she made her way to the back to change.

Davina tapped my shoulder. "We can twin. Don't worry." I gave Davina a big grin as I clapped my hands together in excitement. She tossed me some clothes. I hopped over the seats to make my way to the back of the car. "Well, we need someone who wouldn't look suspicious to go in there," Calvin said, as his eyes went to Octavia. Before you knew it, everyone's eyes went to Octavia. Octavia noticed we were all staring. **"Oh, come on**, why do I always have to be the bate?" Davina and Klaus both looked at each other and shrugged their shoulders comically.

I held back my laughter as Calvin continued to make his point. "Because you're the only one that looks like an *actual* real-life Barbie doll, Octavia." "Alright guys, hurry up. We gotta get to the safe house before dark." Aaminah said as she fixed her hair in the mirror. "And besides, you're the only one that won't get racially profiled," Klaus added as he buckled up his belt.

Octavia rolled her eyes and made her way to the back. "There's not even any… you gotta be kidding me." Octavia went under the seat and pulled out a big pink bag. "If there are pink heels and a dress in here, I'm jumping off the interstate."

Octavia dug in the bag as we all watched intensely. "I bet you two skittles that there's gonna be a whole Barbie starter kit in there." Davina jokingly said to Calvin. Octavia dug deeper and deeper. Suddenly, she just dumped everything out. A huge wad of cash fell out, along with two glocks and a pair of light pink high heels. Everyone gasped in shock as Calvin rushed to the wad of cash.

"What type of female-owned this car?" Klaus picked up one of the guns and popped open the bullet slots. "It's fully loaded." Calvin shook his head. "No way." Calvin grabbed the other gun and checked the bullet slot. "We have two fully loaded guns." Calvin's face filled with excitement. Davina sat up and checked under her seat. She pulled out a bright, sparkly silk dress and a white handbag. Davina held the purse up in the air. "I call dibs on any cash in here."

She dumped everything out. A glittery Victoria Secret makeup bag fell out along with another wad of cash. I couldn't believe my eyes; people from earth were *loaded*. "Oh, my gosh, we're driving a car of a criminal," Octavia mumbled under her breath. Davina began to braid cornrows in my hair as I tied my shoelaces. Aaminah looks at the cash and guns. She looked worried. "The license plate to the car has probably been broadcast on the news by now." Klaus tucked the gun in his pocket. "I'll keep this one." Aaminah laughed. "Have you ever shot a gun before?"

Octavia reached over to Klaus and took the gun out of his hands. "Leave this to the experts," Octavia said as she put the gun in her new pink bag. Calvin laughed. "Man, aren't you full of surprises," Calvin responded, grabbing Octavia's nose. "Touch me again and break your fingers," Octavia scoffed at Calvin. Davina faced me and put a baseball cap on my head. "There you go, now you'll never be found." Calvin turned around. He took one look at me and shook his head. "Why do you look like every Asian rapper that ever lived?"

Klaus held back his laughter. I shook my head and answered back. "Why, you're scared I'll pull more girls than you?" The whole car reacted. "You always got something smart to say, Calvin," Aaminah sighed, putting away the rest of the clothes. I looked back at Davina. I watched Davina as she slicked her puffy mane down and managed to achieve a braided ponytail. "Thank you." I thanked Davina as I got up. Davian just laughed and continued to braid her hair. "No need to thank me, Mazikeen. We're like sisters."

I smiled. I wanted to read her mind to know what she *really* thought of me. You see, until now, nobody knew that I could do this. No one ever knew what I was capable of. Every smart comment, every rude remark that you're thinking, I can hear it. But the funny thing is, I could never hear what my dad was thinking. With my mother, yes, but never with my dad. It was the strangest thing, almost like… I don't know, almost like he didn't want me to hear him thinking. Maybe he just never thought anything at all.

That urge crosses my mind every time someone shows me kindness. But I know it's for the best not to give in to my ability all the time. If I did, I don't think I would have made it out of that space station. That would mean that the demons coming after us would win, and I'm not giving up that easily. If the world is coming to an end, it means I'm finally going to have my beginning. Earth, you are *truly* epic. Whatever Gods plan is for us, I trust it. It's time to show these demons what we're made of. It's go time. **Let's do this.**

Acknowledgments

Being so young and wanting to become an author was not easy for me. I've had lots of sleepless nights. I've really grown as a person doing what I love most. This book has helped me learn more about myself, and it has helped me to inspire others. I proudly dedicate this page to the people in my life who made this process easier to bear and helped me through the tough times when I had my doubts.

I'd like to extend my gratitude to my dear sweet mother. She was with me through this process, and she gave me the strength to keep moving. All the love and support she showers me with means the world to me.

I'd also like to thank my brothers for reading my book and giving me tips on how to improve my storyline. Next, I'd like to thank my older sister for being there to go over my writing and fix my spelling errors.

My largest gratitude goes out to my publisher, who was patient with me and took the time to read my book and publish it. You are the reason why others get to enjoy my work, and I am forever thankful for that.

Last, but certainly not least, I'd like to thank you, my friends, for being there on the phone with me and keeping me up so I could put my all into this book. You guys honestly mean the world to me. Thank you so much to all the wonderful people who motivated me and encouraged me to follow my dreams. You all are truly phenomenal.

About the author

Tiffany Ngwashi is a 15-year-old high school student who enjoys bringing her creations to life. She is an aspiring actress who is filled with ambition. She dreams of publishing 20 books by the time she's 40 and hopes to have at least to become a New York Times Best Sellers. Tiffany lives in Florida with her mother and her two younger twin brothers. Her family is originally from Cameroon and is currently living in the United States of America

This novel is the first book in her book series. Hopefully, this book will be her **Birth of a Book Series.**

www.ingramcontent.com/pod-product-compliance
Lightning Source LLC
Chambersburg PA
CBHW060559190726
48283CB00003B/1078